BBC

National
Short Story
Award 2020

with Cambridge University

First published in Great Britain in 2020 by Comma Press.
www.commapress.co.uk

'The Grotesques' by Sarah Hall was first published in *Sudden Traveller* (Faber & Faber, 2019). 'Scrimshaw' by Eley Williams was first published in *Still Worlds Turning* (No Alibis Press, 2019).

A CIP catalogue record of this book is available
from the British Library.

ISBN-10: 1912697351
ISBN-13: 978-1-91269-735-9

The publisher gratefully acknowledges the support
of Arts Council England.

Printed and bound in Great Britain by Clays Ltd, Elcograf S.p.A

Contents

Introduction

You could make a case that the miniaturist is the aristocrat of artists. Their ability to condense, to compress, to capture a universe in the palm of a hand: it's enough to make you gasp. The precision, control and sheer technical skill required to render the world on a tiny canvas can induce disbelief even that such a thing is possible.

The writers of short stories are literature's miniaturists, imposing on themselves a constraint that makes an already difficult job even harder. To see them achieve over a few thousand words what a novelist might take ten times that number to pull off – creating rounded characters, describing a social world, asking an intriguing question – induces a particular kind of pleasure. It begins with incredulity that they've done it at all.

It's not just readers who feels this way. Even the most accomplished novelists tip their hat to the writer of a good short story. Gabriel García

Márquez once spoke of the difficulty he had writing the first paragraph of a new novel. 'I have spent many months on a first paragraph,' he confessed, explaining that it's in those opening lines that 'the theme is defined, the style, the tone. 'That's why writing a book of short stories is much more difficult than writing a novel. Every time you write a short story, you have to begin all over again.'

Still, readers don't come to short stories to marvel at the technical prowess of the writer. They come to be told a story. Long before I had a clue what was involved in the making of such fiction, I lapped it up. I'd not long graduated from *Charlie and the Chocolate Factory* and *Danny the Champion of the World* when I made the transition to Roald Dahl's stories for adults. They were dark and delicious, with the guaranteed satisfaction of an often-macabre twist, but above all they promised the pleasure of *being told a story*.

Here the brevity is crucial. Few readers can complete a novel in a single sitting, but a short story demands to be digested that way. The result is that the reading of short fiction resembles the ancient, maybe even primal, experience of being sat down as someone tells you a tale. You begin it together and end it together; nothing gets in the way. There's no getting off at the next stop or turning off the bedside light. For that period – ten minutes or the best part of an hour – the storyteller has you in their grasp.

For this year's BBC National Short Story Award with Cambridge University, we were transported to dystopian futures and unresolved pasts, from Africa to Belarus, from inner London to the outest of Hebrides. We heard lost languages and lost music, tasted the sweet melancholy of first love and the pain of unhealed grief – each of these encounters taking place over the number of pages that might make up a modest book chapter. The writing was inventive and dexterous, occasionally funny, often moving. If this year's entries are anything to go by, the short story – a form too often written off - is in vibrant health.

It fell to five of us – Lucy Caldwell, Irenosen Okojie, Chris Power, Di Speirs and me – to harvest from this bumper crop just five stories. We had no set criteria; there were no boxes we wanted to tick. For my own part, I asked only that I be taken away by the writing. And I was.

'In the Car with the Rain Coming Down' by Jan Carson is about nothing more dramatic than a thwarted family picnic in the Northern Irish countryside. It is the world of a bag of Percy Pigs and The Carpenters on the radio. Yet it has moments of pathos and comedy where each note rings true: the tiny slights, the invisible hierarchies, the disappointments that contour any family. There wasn't a huge amount of humour in this year's entries – perhaps a reflection of these sombre times – but Carson's story made more than one judge laugh out loud, perhaps in recognition. The story is tender, humane and satisfying, written in an unflashy prose that prefers to draw attention to its characters than to itself.

'The Grotesques' also depicts a family, through the eyes of a writer, Sarah Hall, who is, to use Saul Bellow's description of himself, 'a first-class noticer.' The lead character is a woman with a pained and unhealthy relationship with food: 'There was an art to second helpings: you had to be confident and move fast, look as if you were helpfully clearing crockery.' Written so elegantly it gleams, this is a story whose evocation of one woman's mental state recalled Virginia Woolf's *Mrs Dalloway* or the stories of Katherine Mansfield. Even those characters who appear only fleetingly have a hinterland; you'd happily press further into their lives, because you believe they have them.

Death lingers in that story, as it does in 'Come Down Heavy' by Jack Houston, written with such brio it could be delivered as a spoken word performance. It takes you to the margins, to those who have been not so much left behind as crushed underfoot. This is a story that could so easily have gone wrong. In less skilled hands, it might have lapsed into voyeurism or poverty porn. Instead, in a form that matched the jumble and chaos of lives broken by addiction, it conveyed truth.

'Scrimshaw' by Eley Williams is a miniature among miniatures, a story so concise it runs for about the length of a newspaper column. And yet in that short span, it establishes a distinct and memorable voice, one that is witty, playful and insightful about what we do with technology and what technology is doing to us: our conversation, our thoughts, our mating rituals. There is emotion and longing too, expressed in 'the trailing three dots' on the screen of a phone, that 21st century signifier of impatience and desire.

The voice is just as distinct and arresting in 'Pray' by Caleb Azumah Nelson, a story that fizzes off the page. The dialogue is immediate, the descriptions authentic. But it's the wisdom that gives 'Pray' its power. 'The world we frequented wasn't built with us in mind,' is a terse distillation of racism. 'We're the wrong age, too young to be adults, too old to be children, but stuck in bodies which implicated us both ways' is a line which captures perfectly a very specific stage of life. The notion that the death of two aged characters 'was their bodies rebelling, finally protesting at the toll the tension of living in our skin takes. Finally showing that there is a breaking point' brims with prescience, given all that this year has brought.

All these gems await you. So sit down, pick one at random, and let five masters of this taut, tight form take you to different worlds, revealed in miniature.

Jonathan Freedland,
London, 2020

Pray

Caleb Azumah Nelson

PRAY FOR AUTUMN. PRAY for Winter. Pray for Spring, for the days rain sneaks under raincoats and we might watch bare trees bear fruit. Pray for Summer to come and go without incident, this Summer where we rage as hot as the red sun at dusk. Pray the young man wasn't your friend, or a friend of a friend. Pray the grief passes. Pray we learn what to do with this anger. Pray for Autumn. Pray for Winter. Pray it is too cold to venture outside. Pray we stay in our yards as the daylight fails, and hold those we love. Pray we are neither hunter, nor prey. Pray we forget, and we come and go as we please, spilling from yard to yard, touching one party only to touch the next. Pray we have forgotten before the first toke, that the smoke which fills our lungs and slows the brain is a pleasure, not a necessity. Pray we forget, but not for too long. Pray for Autumn. Pray for Winter. Pray for Spring. Pray we don't suppress the fear. Pray the ache stops. Pray.

It is summer again, and it's 2008. I've got my hoody on – the Black Nike one, with the metal tips swinging from the drawstrings. We all do, our hoods up because we don't know when the skies might open over our heads.

In summer, we plot. We gather with no specific purpose. It's a kind of protest, a reaching towards a freedom we don't often encounter but believe we deserve. We go wherever this freedom can be housed, which tends to be in parks and open spaces, kicking a flat football across a caged play area, daring gravity to meet us as we commandeer swings or tiny merry-go-rounds. This year, we have been hanging out by the unmoving stream which runs around the back of Catford. We're rarely less than five on these evenings, where the dying sunlight creeps towards us, dousing all in a pink glow. We eat and we drink. We wobble across the water's edge, like we're fearless.

'Watch out, man, be easy!' We can fault Rodney's neuroses, his need for order and control, but never his outfit choice. He's got Nike on too, hoody and the bottoms which taper towards the ankles, highlighting the white pair of Air Forces on his feet. He's protesting at the crusty football we're passing between us, and the flecks of dirt which fly with each touch.

'Don't be such a baby, it's just a little dirt,' Paul says, rolling the ball in his direction. Rodney lets out a little yelp, darting a short distance away, towards safety. We all fall about, Paul, Daniel, Eric, James, my older brother Christopher and myself, that kind of laughter which renders you breathless. A sullen Rodney perches on a bit of concrete, inspecting his trainers for dark spots.

'You man have no respect,' he says, sulking. '"*Treddin' on Thin Ice*".'

'Rodney, come on, man. Come with something else, your dead bars,' Eric says.

'They're not even mine.'

'Nah, you're right, fam. Your dead *recycled* bars.'

'What you saying about Wiley? I'm East, bruv.'

'Yeah but you're in South now,' says Christopher.

This, too, is a familiar routine. Rodney's undying devotion to E3, Bow Road, and everything East; the rest of us, local, unrelenting, sure that South East is where our world begins and ends.

'These ends are so dead,' Rodney begins.

'Then leave,' Eric says. 'You're a big man. You work, I know you've got p's 'cause you're always looking nice. Always complaining. What's keeping you here?'

'My Dad,' Rodney says, rolling a stone underfoot. This quietens us. We all know that

Rodney's dad has long begun to forget, or perhaps it is the things he remembers which cause him to stutter and shake. Rodney and his twin sister, Ife, take care of him in two-day swings. I went to check Rodney last year, when they first moved to Bellingham. His father was sat at the kitchen table, wearing his dressing gown and a kufi cap. He was engaged in a game of chess, in which he appeared to be playing himself, locked in stalemate. I watched as Rodney, too, forgot himself, watching his father, searching for a version of the man that he, too, was in danger of forgetting.

Daniel lights a joint, puffs without hands, and coughs into the silence. He passes it to Rodney, who accepts, and says, 'The girls, as well.' Murmurs and smiles, all round.

'South girls are just better,' I say, without thinking.

'What you know about *women*, little man?' Eric asks.

All attention diverts toward me. I fold inwards with its weight. The joint has made its way from Daniel to Rodney, to Eric, who lets out a plume of smoke into the sky. Paul grows bored of waiting and plays with the ball at his feet. Eric inhales again, and pushes his point.

'Tell us then? What you know?'

'Tell them about Tamika,' Christopher says.

'Tamika? That's what's-her-names sister? What's her name?' Eric taps Rodney.

'Why you hitting me, man, I don't know –'

'Lizzie! She's kinda nice, still. So wagwan for you and her sister?'

The attention returns, and I smile a little. I want to tell them what I had told Christopher in our kitchen, last week. That, on the last day of sixth form, Tamika had taken my hand, and led me through one door, then another, into a short dimly lit passageway leading towards the library. She pulled me close and grazed her nose against mine, her lips running across my cheek, under my chin, the short crevice where neck meets head.

'Hey,' she said, not pausing.

'Mm-hm?'

'Do you like me?'

I stepped back a little here, and meeting her eyes, nodded. She smiled.

'Don't look so scared. I like you, too.'

My hands slid down the delicate curve of her back, down, down, down; her hands reached for my back too, but her fingers crept under my shirt, each one finding brief purchase against skin flush with summer heat. A fingertip brushed the narrow passage between my shoulder blades and that's when I kissed her, her lips parting slightly as they met mine. Time stopped, or rather time passed, and we stopped regarding it. Our hands moved in a flurry. When the school bell rang, it was almost welcome. Facing each other, the tension snapped, and all we could do was laugh.

When I return from the memory, the whole group is waiting expectantly.

'I lipsed her. In the library,' I add.

'Are you mad! Young Einstein over here, lipsing girls in the library. My guy.'

Rodney lowers his voice an octave, impersonating my baritone thrum. '*I seen you, and I was just wondering if you wanted to come to my yard and see my book collection.*'

And it's here, as we sit kicking back by the water's edge, wearing dusk like a light coat; here, as I recall the memory of being lost with another, in another; here, as we fall about laughing at the absurdity of it all, this life we have been given, that we can be free – even if it does not last.

Our parents had always told us home was somewhere we could be free, too. Two bedrooms, a bathroom Mum had insisted we clean after every shower, a kitchen forever in use, something was always on the stove, jollof, or plantain sputtering in the pot, aloe vera plant on the windowsill Christopher and I never watered, forever living, dying, living. The living room the centrepiece, cavernous room with the HiFi system Dad claimed to have used to DJ at a venue which had long closed down, the cupboard full of records, a home made from rhythm, space large enough for us all to move around in, like those Sundays, in the long lull between a late breakfast and an early dinner, nibbling on crisps and peanuts, Dad, now out of his church wear, sporting a Guinness and white vest, Mum entertaining him as he crooned along to Teddy Pendergrass, maybe a little Marvin, New Edition if he made it to his second Guinness, Boyz II Men if he made it to his third. Dad was a silly, mournful drunk, starting stories he couldn't finish, always asking Mum if she remembered, did she remember? She would smile at this man, their rhythms the same, really, slow, so slow and contemplative.

Those Sundays were wonderful. Christopher and I would watch our jolly father drink himself towards a nap, Mum so exhausted she didn't need the aid, tucking in beside him on the sofa. Christopher would turn the heat down on the food, and we fled to our room. No sooner had I clicked the door shut was Christopher kneeling by our small boombox, riffling through the pouch of CDs we had burned during the week at the library. If it was summer 2006, then Dizzee was still in rotation, our 50 Cent obsession hadn't waned, and I was still arguing that Nas was better than Jay. Christopher and I both agreed that Biggie was the better rapper than Tupac, but Pac had something else, something you couldn't hold or give words to, something deliberate. A feeling. Kano dropped the year before, and we talked about that thing that he had, that they all had, that we all had, that feeling, the men and women we heard through our speakers riding over sixteen bar counts deliberate in their being; knowing that to look like we did, the choice had to be deliberate, because the world we frequented wasn't built with us in mind.

We had the sitting on a Friday. Uncle Robert and Auntie Grace came over in the morning, helping us to hollow out the room. We took Dad's HiFi and speakers out, so all that was left was silence. The sudden emptiness was similar to the rapid decline our parents undertook, the cancers somehow burrowing through them both in one short year. Auntie Grace didn't think it was fast, or a coincidence. She was sure it was their bodies rebelling, finally protesting at the toll the tension of living in our skin takes. Finally showing that there is a breaking point.

   That morning, they set up folding chairs on the edges of the room, thrusting the large windows open, a soft breeze billowing through the room. Before the guests arrived, I called my own name, the way my parents had in the months before they became too weak to do so, and heard my own voice as someone else might for the first time, the low timbre trembling, tender with loss.

Those of my parents' siblings who lived in this country arrived first, taking up the sofa and seats adjacent. My father's family came *en masse*, draped in black funeral cloth, accented by red scarves, this colour particular to my family. As each guest arrived, relative and non-relative, they would make their way around the room, shaking the hand of each sibling, paying their respects. A prayer followed, delivered by the eldest sibling, asking for blessing, even as my parents had departed. The mood lifted a little after this. Heaving plates of rice and chicken were served, and someone brought up their own sound equipment, placing it in the hallway, so that highlife filled the flat.

I watched Christopher for most of the afternoon. Watched everyone approach him, as they were approaching me, extending condolences and sorrow for our loss. Late in the day, I saw him grow tired and snap. I guess, like me, he was tired of being asked to stuff the well wishes and conciliations into a hole, widened by grief, which couldn't be filled. When he slipped out of the flat, I followed.

I found him outside with our Uncle Robert and a group of men, family friends around the same age, laughing as they poured him a healthy measure of a brown spirit. Christopher passed me his own cup, and motioned they pour him another.

'How old are you?' One of the men asked me.

'He's old enough,' Christopher said.

We all sipped deeply, wincing as the liquid surged down our throats. I resisted the urge to cough.

'Uncle Rob, what is this?' I asked.

'*Forget-me-not*. This one, when you take a sip, you don't forget what it tastes like,' he said, heaving with laughter. His body convulsed with each sharp rumble, shaking and shifting until I was unsure of what his tears meant. He looked up and out – we all did, following his gaze – at a pair of children, distant relations, as they breached the boundary of the car they were emerging from, running, running, running, letting out yelps of delight. Uncle Rob looked down at the ground.

'My only sister,' he said, his eyes glistening. He turns to me, then Christopher. 'It's just you two now, you know?' The other men murmur in agreement.

That same night, when the guests began to dwindle, I slipped away to our bedroom. The day knocked me flat and I lay on the bed, gazing at the ceiling, not asleep but not conscious either, floating in a place so lucid I could feel my body willing itself on, willing itself to live.

'Oi.'

Christopher was at the foot of the bed, taking off his black shirt, throwing on a black hoody.

'You look mashed,' he said.

'Trust.'

'What you telling me, you tryna roll?'

I propped myself up on my elbows, watching as he stepped into the matching tracksuit bottoms.

'Where?' I asked.

'Out. You're coming anyway, bruv. It's just me and you now.' He chucked my hoody at me, and I rose, willing myself on.

We bumped the train a few stops, from Bellingham to Peckham Rye, nodding at the gate attendant as we pushed through the side gate.

'Come,' Christopher said to me, pulling up his hood as he led me along Rye Lane. We're the wrong age, too young to be adults, too old be children, but stuck in bodies which implicated us both ways. The street was heaving. At any time of day, this stretch of road was pedestrianised: people on their way to raves and drink ups, parents leading their tired children to another family function, young women with their hair just done, an older uncle trying to get home. Young men like us with their hoods up for safety, for comfort in the semi-darkness. Raucous laughter as the day begins to stretch into another, whole groups plotting, trying to figure out if it's worth switching postcodes for a party where tedium, or something worse, might lie in wait. And Christopher and I, making our way around the curve of the road, hoping no one takes exception, hoping if we walk with enough purpose we might reach our destination.

At least, that's how I felt. Christopher never appeared scared, always with his chin raised a little higher than mine, his chest puffed, not boastfully, but with a confidence, a conviction, a truth.

We continued on, passing Commercial Way and onto Southampton Way, roads our parents would only let us pass in a car. On and on, onto a side road, into an industrial estate, where I heard the crowd before I saw them. Christopher approached a door cut into an enormous shutter, and knocked once, twice.

The door swung open and we were pulled into a sweatbox. There were fifty or so people in a space for twenty-five, but somehow Christopher pulled me through the crowd to the front, where

Paul, Daniel, Eric and James waited, all blacked out too from head to toe, James wearing a beanie hat and a North Face jacket.

'Aren't you hot, fam?' I asked

'Aesthetic, init,' he said, as we all embraced each other.

'How many mics we got?' Christopher asked.

'Two,' Eric said, raising a pair of black microphones in hand.

'Alright, calm. Let's go then.'

'Oi, careful tonight,' Daniel said. 'Trev and them man are here.'

Christopher's face hardened for a flash, before that smile I know so well returned. He gestured to us all to get started, and I made towards the crowd, taking two small but distinct steps back.

'Where you going? Come stand with us, bro.'

'I can't.'

'What you mean?'

'I didn't know you were doing this tonight. You know I don't have it like you do.' Though I was sure I had rhythm, that I could make a sentence curve to my will, this theory was untested in public and I worried I would flounder under the pressure. Christopher and I would often descend into absurd freestyles on our Sunday afternoons, going back to back, bar for bar, gassing each other when a line would emerge, seemingly from nowhere, that would make us stop in wonder, processing the phrase from all angles. But here? I shook my head.

'Nah, nah. No one's making you step to the mic unless you really want to.' I shook my head again. He wrapped his arm around my shoulders and pulled me close so that his lips brushed my ear as he spoke. 'You're here to be part of this. For the vibe. For the hype.' He paused. 'You're here to enjoy yourself. Shit hasn't been fun of late. This is where I come for a little fun. Can you do that for me? Have some fun?'

I nodded, and we bumped fists. We separated and he flicked the mic on, bringing it to his mouth, calling for attention in the room. Everyone was silent as Christopher introduced himself and our crew. When he told the DJ, posted up on a makeshift table in the far corner of the room, to start spinning, the silence morphed to quiet, which is a different thing altogether, and requires a very specific attention. The crowd latched onto Christopher's energy as his tongue danced over sparse instrumentals, heavy with snares and kicks and hi-hats, nothing that would muddy his vocals. He took the time with each syllable, even as he worked himself up, even as it appeared he was careening, matching the crowd's energy, them matching his, this dance accentuated by the nodding of heads, the encouraging shouts in our direction. After the third song, he took a moment.

'Are you man ready?' Christopher addressed the crowd. He turned to us, still speaking into the mic. 'I don't think they're ready.' The crowd protested, pressing forward. They were hungry. 'Come then, run it up one time.'

The beat started and knocked me back. The crowd surged forward as the bass rattled our bones, a kick sneaking amongst the rattle of the hi-hats. The snare was so bare it resembled a clap. We're moving, we're all moving, and I was pulled into the moshpit, arms and hands and legs swinging. We had relinquished control. We were the words unspoken. We were joyous. We were an ocean that we had chosen to jump into, rather than being thrown overboard. I caught a glimpse of Christopher in the moment before he started rapping. He was a man possessed, or rather a man in full possession of himself. He delivered his lyrics with the precision of a poet: *We hurt people 'cah we been hurt too/Cause trust me I don't wanna hurt you/But I know when this anger gets loose/It might find a home in your front tooth*. And as he took a deep inhale, ready to swing with his next line, the DJ spun the track back, cutting the music, and to the glee of the crowd, Christopher lowered his microphone, taking this all in, grinning.

In the police and news reports, they will describe Christopher as though he never had a beginning. That he appeared, whole and black and mean and threatening. To take someone's beginning is to render him null and void, to suggest his rhythm doesn't exist. But man, does Christopher have rhythm. He's stiff and slow and subtle with it, his walk like a dance, a glide, a waltz. He's only a year older than me, a year and some change, but older than me in ways we can't describe. It is a grown man's rhythm, sensitive and understanding, stubborn and talented, complex – eternally complex.

On the weekends, he transforms our living room into a makeshift studio, dragging his recording equipment into the space. People come in and out while Christopher sits listening to Nina and Billie and Ella, listening for phrases he can sample, that he can cut and stretch into something new, something he can loop and leave while people step up to the mic. We lounge and dance and whoop and laugh, smoking and drinking ourselves into a beautiful frenzy, carried by the music, carried by what comes towards us but cannot be explained. Christopher smokes until his eyes crack red. He likes wine, too. He likes to slow down his pace, his racing heart. He likes to be on his own time.

Sometimes, this frenetic fervour becomes too much. Sometimes, Christopher is disturbed, like the time someone bumped the record player while Miles' trumpet crooned. The needle scratched the record, the rhythm broke, a flash of something, a stony face, his eyes narrow, a strength in his legs, tense, taut arms, a bellowed question, who did that? Who did that? Everyone talking him down from a ledge we're all standing on, some less securely than others. We're talking him down, knowing that we would want the same, knowing no one wants to fall, no one wants to be consumed.

Sometimes, I catch Christopher praying. It'll be nighttime, midweek, and I'll stir from sleep. I'll hear him asking to be delivered from evil. To banish this anger. To protect us from what we can't see but know lurks in the air. Dull the sour paranoia on his tongue. Forgive him for reaching for the smoke. Forgive him for reaching for the bottle. Deliver him from evil. Asking how he got here. Asking if he's good. Asking if he's cursed.

Asking for peace.

It's 2008, and summer is almost over. Christopher returns home not long after I do. It's Sunday, so he's been at the studio. I've been with Tamika. She and I have been seeing each other since the school year finished, floating together through this limbo before university starts. Earlier, we were stumbling back to her flat, having spent the day at someone's free house, getting through the bottle of rum we brought and then some.

'I love this, you know,' she said. 'I love this so much.'

'So do I,' I said, our arms snaking around each other's waists, holding each other up.

'I know we're young, and like, yeah. Yeah.' She sighed wistfully. 'I feel safe here, you know?'

I nodded. She was right. Tamika and I have become lost in each other, in this feeling, in this safety, and it has filled the loss which hasn't stopped at my parents, or her eldest brother, Kweku, or Brian, who was the year above us at school, or Tej, who, after Brian, could not see anything further than retaliation, and lost himself in this act. This loss, this incomprehensible loss, steals bodies in the night, leaving ghosts and shells behind. I saw Brian's mother a few days after the funeral, and it was like whatever hand had struck Brian had taken the same tool and hollowed her out, too. Her words were incoherent. She was at a loss, she was lost, she was in danger of being no more.

I hear the door catch as I wait for the kettle to boil. I'm sparring with the beginnings of a hangover, and I can already hear my brother's gentle ribbing: *This guy. Out drinking again? Nah, nah, I'm not judging you, fam. But you'll do anything for girl, init?*

When he does walk into the kitchen, there's blood on his shirt.

'What happened? Bro, what happened?'

He's shaking his head. His words are incoherent. He is lost, he is at a loss, he is in danger of being no more. I check his person. I pull off his shirt, his arms limp like a tired child. He is unhurt physically but his body is crumbling. He can barely stand. He is floating, a ghost, a shell. It does not look like his body is willing itself to live.

'Christopher!' The sharpness catches him, draws his attention.

'I don't even know. I don't even know.' He's shaking his head again. He looks at me and what is left of him breaks. 'He came out of nowhere. Like he'd been waiting for me. *Fuck*. I hit him so hard.' He looks straight at me. 'Talk to me, man. I'm bugging out, talk to me.'

I don't have the words. I don't have the words, so I take my brother in my arms, pull him in while the tears fall down our faces. I hold him for a moment. I leave the kitchen and pull a chair into the room. I sit him down. I leave again. I return with a damp flannel and a fresh shirt. I wipe his face and underneath his chin. I tell him to raise his arms, and slip the shirt on over his head. I don't know what compels me, but I place my hand on his head, rubbing his hair with my thumb.

'You got a fade,' I say. He nods smiling, he nods and gazes down. He begins to cry again, and I wipe away each fresh tear as it comes.

I talk to him like nothing has happened, like nothing has changed. It's just us two now.

'You should've come Church. Auntie Grace was killing me through the sermon.'

'What was the sermon about?

'Cain and Abel. You ever read that?' He nods. 'It got me thinking though. The focus is always on Cain killing his brother, and then Cain being killed with this same stone. But I'm sitting there today, thinking, who put the stone in his hand in the first place? I don't think we were born violent.' I pause. 'You hungry?'

He nods through the tears. It's Sunday, and I reach into the fridge for the Tupperware. I prepare a plate of food for him, and one for myself. It's just us two. We eat until we're full, filling our empty bodies, willing ourselves to live.

In the Car with the Rain Coming Down

Jan Carson

THERE'S A STAND-OFF IN the front yard. No
significant progress can be made until the men
decide who's driving. It's the same every time we
go anywhere together.

There are six cars in the yard. To say they've
been parked would be giving the drivers too
much credit. They look as if they've been
dropped from a great height and have come to
rest at outlandish angles, sniffing each other's
bumpers like a pack of frisky dogs. The men are
debating which cars will be required today.
They've ruled out Matty's wee Nova. He's taken
the backseat out for transporting feed. The
whole car stinks of sheep and teenage boy. You
wouldn't want to be cooped up in it; not in this
clammy heat. The Escort's out too. It's filthy with
dog hair. William, my father-in-law, keeps it for

his collies. He's never once thought of cleaning it out. Sure, what would be the point? This leaves four cars in the running: Brian's big Audi, our - more modest - Audi, Cathy's Golf and the Peugeot 407 William keeps for driving Susan to church on Sundays. It will require two cars to transport us all. We are nine these days; soon to be ten. Next time we head out together we might need a third car. Baby seats take up a lot of space.

The men have distanced themselves from the women. They have their hands in their pockets, jiggling keys. They're not looking at each other. They are intentional about this. William has a suit jacket on, a dress shirt and tie. I recognise this get up. He used to wear it to church a few years back. It has seen better days. The elbows are shiny from being leant on. There's a button missing from the cuff. It's still too formal for a day like today. He'll be sweltered. He won't be able to kick football with the boys. The boys have made no such effort. Buff and Brian are in T-shirts and tracksuit bottoms. Matty's wearing a pair of shorts, a branded polo and hoodie, knotted loosely round his shoulders. He's taken to wearing his shirt collar up, copying the lads at the Rugby Club. He's the youngest; the only one still living at home. Surrounded by his sons, in their trainers, William looks stiff and faded, like a man lifted from another time.

William insists he will drive. Brian is equally insistent that he won't.

'It's your birthday, Dad,' he says. 'Let us chauffeur you about for a change.'

Young William, (or Buff, as we call him), says, 'I don't mind driving either.'

He says this so quietly nobody hears. I hear. He's my husband. I'm used to him. Even so, I miss half the things he says. Buff's a wild mumbler. Susan once told me he had a speech impediment when he was younger. He's never told me this himself. That's not to say it isn't true. There are lots of things Buff doesn't tell me. He's not having affairs or gambling or anything like that. It's the embarrassing things he keeps to himself. Diarrhoea. Parking tickets. The time he tripped over the entrance mat in Tesco's and fell into a stack of cereal packets. I only heard about that because Jill next door was coming through the door behind him.

I'd like my husband to be more assertive, especially around his family, but it doesn't come natural to him. I shout across the yard, 'Buff could drive, so he could. We're only after filling the car up.' Sometimes, I have to do the asserting for him.

We women are standing at the door. We are glaring at the men. All five of us are wearing versions of the same thing: cut-off trousers, a T-shirt, sandals and some sort of cardigan. Susan's swapped her cut-offs for a calve-length skirt: mint green with cream and blue brushstrokes running across it in waves. I've never once seen my mother-in-law in trousers. I don't think she owns any. We women are losing patience with the men. We are clucking and fussing like caged chickens. There's a fresh cream sponge to be considered. It'll be going off in this heat.

'Don't be causing a scene, William,' shouts Susan. 'Just let the boys drive.'

William turns to look at his wife. He raises a hand to her.

'Wheesht, Susan,' he says.

I've seen him pull the same move with cows.

Susan rolls her eyes. She mutters something under her breath. It could be *amen*, – for she's a very religious woman – or it could just as easily be, *men*. My money's on the latter. It wouldn't be the first time I've heard her snap at William; only under her breath, of course. She'd never let him hear her giving cheek. She smooths the pink anorak which is draped over her forearm. Even on a warm day like today, Susan considers it tempting fate to leave home without an anorak.

When this anorak's not hooked round her handbag strap, she carries it in front of her, like a wine waiter's towel, shielding her belly and upper thighs. Susan is the sort of woman who doesn't like to be seen. This is not to say Susan doesn't see absolutely everything. She's like God himself; you couldn't get anything by her. She glances upwards now, past Brian's wife, Michelle, and the monkey puzzle tree which dominates the front lawn.

'There's a cloud,' she announces solemnly. 'It's going to rain if we don't get a move on.'

I squint at the sky, angling my eyes north towards the coast where we'll be heading as soon as the car situation's sorted. Sure enough, there is a cloud – a single, fist-sized puff of white – interrupting the blue.

'Uch, it's only a wee cloud, Susan,' I say. 'I think we'll be grand.'

My sister-in-law, Cathy and her partner glance at each other and smile. The pair of them are always getting on like this. Smiling. Touching. Kissing each other in unusual places such as shoulders and earlobes. They are stupid happy. I wouldn't want to be a lesbian myself, but I envy Cathy all the same. Buff's never looked at me the way Clodagh looks at her; not even at the start, when we were shifting, secretly, behind the chicken sheds. Back then, Buff said we were like

25

Kate Winslet and your man in *Titanic* and I said that was a very romantic thing to say, (which, for Buff, it really was), though I couldn't, for the life of me, see the similarity. *Romeo and Juliet* would've been a better comparison, but Buff hadn't seen the film of it.

Cathy and Clodagh have piled all our picnic stuff up against the wall. They're standing in the middle of the mess, holding hands, waiting to see which cars to put it in. Cool boxes, biscuit tins, deck chairs and rugs are all stacked next to the enormous thermos flasks Susan's borrowed from the church. One's filled with tea. The other's got plain hot water in it because she prefers Nescafe with her sandwiches.

Michelle's done a Victoria sponge. She's already made a palaver of lifting it out of the boot. 'Don't be looking too closely, ladies,' she said, opening the cake tin and shoving it right under her mother-in-law's nose. 'I literally flung this together last night. It's like a dog's dinner.' Dog's dinner, my arse. Michelle's cake is like something you'd see in the *Bake Off* final. I've not bothered baking myself. Since the baby, I haven't been able to. The very sight of a raw egg turns me. It's the slime I can't be doing with; the way the white clings to the shell like loose snot. I've bought all our picnic stuff from Marks and Spencer's.

Correction: Buff's bought everything from Marks and Spencer's. I gave him a list. He's good like that; offering before I have to ask. I can tell he'll be hands-on with the baby too. He's as excited as I am, in his own Buffy sort of way.

Susan's just noticed the Marks and Spencer's bag. She pokes at it with the toe of her pewter sandal. She's made an effort for William's birthday. Her toenails are painted pink to match her fingernails, though the effect's muted by a layer of nylon tights: bamboo colour with a thick seam cutting across her nails.

'It's nice for some,' she says. 'I wish I could afford to buy everything out of Marksy's.'

'Sorry,' I say, 'I've been that busy with work.'

I've no idea why I'm apologising. I just am.

Clodagh hears us. She catches my eye and smiles kindly. I wonder if she already knows; if Buff's told Cathy, and Cathy's told Clodagh, and the word's already out. We'd agreed we were going to tell the whole family together; this afternoon, after the birthday cake. I smile back at Clodagh. She rolls her eyes in Susan's direction. She mouths the word, *bitch*. I almost laugh out loud. No, I decide, Clodagh doesn't know. She's just being nice. She can't stand Susan either.

I like Clodagh a lot. She's fit right in with the rest of us. Granted, the older generation's a bit stiff around her. Susan calls her *Catherine's wee friend* and William will up and leave the room if they're sitting too close or holding hands. But neither of them will ever say anything to the girls. They're too scared of where the conversation might lead. You start being honest with each other and it's like opening *what's her name's box*. You never know what'll come slinking out. Despite the politeness, you can tell they'd prefer it if Clodagh was somebody else: a man, ideally. It's not just the lesbian thing that's grating on them. Clodagh's the other sort too. Her family's from Letterkenny. They've a hardware shop down there, in the Free State, as Susan insists upon calling it. You have to give the girl her dues. She has some balls, taking up with the likes of Cathy. I've no notion how they met. Before Clodagh, Cathy only ever brought farmers home: big, pink-faced lads with bootcut jeans and Caterpillar boots. God knows, where she fell in with a lesbian. I was grateful when she did. I thought it'd take the heat off me. It didn't. There's a pecking order when it comes to my mother-in-law's affections. Even lesbian lovers rate higher than me.

Clodagh bends down and peers into the open-mouth of the Marks and Spencer's bag. She sticks her hand in, rifles around and emerges with a packet of Percy Pigs.

'Good woman, Vicky,' she says, beaming up at me. 'These are like, my all-time favourite sweeties.'

'They totally are,' confirms Cathy. 'That one'll do anything for a Percy Pig.'

'Anything,' says Clodagh, flashing Cathy a very suggestive look. 'Here, what would you do for a Percy Pig, Sue?' she asks, waggling the packet under my mother-in-law's nose.

Susan is flustered. She knows she's being mocked. She just doesn't know how to respond.

'No thank you,' she says. She slips a second arm under her folded anorak and pulls it towards herself defensively.

Clodagh continues to wave the Percy Pigs about. She's doing a funny dance, wiggling her backside as she emits a series of snuffly pig noises. Cathy is cracking up. I am cracking up. Susan is trying to smile and not quite managing it and holding her anorak so tightly it's going to need ironing later. She'd like to be in on the joke, but she doesn't know what the joke is. She looks towards Michelle, hoping she'll wade in and help. But Michelle is on her knees checking the state of her Victoria Sponge. (Not good. Not good at all. The whole thing's started to slide in the heat).

'It's going to rain,' Susan announces abruptly. 'We need to get going.' An edge of panic has crept into her voice. It sticks a little on the third syllable so *to* and *rain* sound strangled, as if she's coughing and speaking at the same time.

Clodagh can see the joke's gone far enough. She stuffs the Percy Pigs into her cardigan pocket.

'Don't be getting your knickers in a twist, Sue,' she says.

She sticks her thumb and index finger into her mouth, forming a circle beneath her tongue. She blows hard. The noise which comes out is somewhere between a wolf whistle and the sound William makes when he's calling the dogs. The men stop talking. They turn to stare at Clodagh.

'Right lads, let's head,' she shouts. 'Buff and Brian should drive. Their cars are bigger.'

It is as if God has spoken. The men stop arguing instantly. They nod at Clodagh and, without saying anything, disperse. I can't decide whether it's the tone she's taken, or the fact that she's an outsider. Surely, it can't be anything to do with her being a lesbian. These men don't usually take instructions from women. I'd be jealous if I wasn't half in love with Clodagh myself. I've known my father-in-law for the better part of two decades and I could never take that tone with him. She's been on the scene for all of five minutes and she's already bossing him about.

William gets into the dog car. He backs it up so there's room for both the Audis to edge past. Brian, Buff and Matty start loading the picnic stuff into the open boots. Clodagh stands in the middle of the yard, directing operations. William and Susan will go with Brian and Michelle; the birthday boy riding up front, next to his son. William gets into the passenger seat immediately. He doesn't even bother offering it to his wife. It's a country thing. You'd not expect a man to sit in the backseat. It wouldn't be dignified.

Our car's not as flashy as Brian's, but it is bigger. We'll take Matty and the girls. It'll be a squeeze but that'll hardly bother Cathy and Clodagh. Matty comes stumbling across the yard with a rug and two deckchairs. 'Shotgun,' he shouts.

Buff lifts the chairs out of his brother's arms and places them inside the boot.

'Do you mind if Vicky sits up front, mate?' he asks. 'She gets a bit bokey in the backseat.'

'Course,' says Matty, 'so long as I'm not stuck between the dykes like a big gooseberry.'

Susan's ears prick up. She pauses – one leg into Brian's Audi, one leg out – and gives Matty a withering look. 'That's no way to talk about your sister and her friend,' she says. 'Show a bit of respect.'

I'm shocked on multiple levels. Mostly, I'm surprised to discover that Susan knows a word like dyke. I wonder where she's heard it. Maybe on Sky. William's finally upgraded to satellite. If you ask William, he'll say the Sky's for the young lad. He'll claim he never watches it himself. Buff says he's hooked on the American programmes. He's big into *How I Met Your Mother*. He has the whole series pre-recorded.

We finish loading up the cars and climb in. Brian sticks his head out the window. I have to open my door to hear him. Our electric windows are on the blink.

'I'll go first,' he shouts across to Buff. 'We'll head for the White Rocks. Keep your phone on, in case there's a change of plan.'

'Ok,' says Buff. I turn to relay this message to Brian. He already has his window up. He revs the Audi and takes off at speed. By the time Buff turns our car and edges carefully down the lane, avoiding the suicidal cats who fling themselves under the wheels of passing cars, Brian's Audi is long gone. He'll be at the White Rocks before we've even made it to Ballymoney. Brian drives like a lunatic.

Buff is careful behind the wheel; cautious even. He passed his test on the third attempt and claims this makes him a better driver. He has never had an accident. At least he's never hit another vehicle. He does have a tendency to drive into stationary objects: bollards, walls, kerbs. He's not good at judging distance – something to do with his prescription lenses – but at least he never goes fast enough to do any real damage. As we drive out of the village and turn on to the dual carriageway he begins to accelerate, slowly and meticulously working his way up through the gears 'til he hits sixty and goes no further.

Matty leans through from the back seat. 'Put the foot down, Buff,' he says. 'You're driving like an old woman.'

'Sixty's fast enough,' says Buff.

'It's not a bloody funeral.'

'I won't be going any faster than sixty, Matthew. If that doesn't suit, you can get out and walk.'

'Naw, mate. I'd be scared of overtaking you.'

He turns to claim a congratulatory high-five off Cathy. She puts him in a headlock instead.

'Leave the Buffster alone,' she says. 'It's not his fault. The oldest sibling's always the sensible one. It's just the way it is.'

'Now Catherine, by sensible do you actually mean boring?' asks Matty, squirming free of her grip.

They're always taking the piss out of Buff. It's usually good-hearted. Sometimes, I even join in. They mock his driving, his dress sense, (which is, to be honest, non-existent), his mumbly way of speaking, his love of The Carpenters. My husband is an easy man to mock. Usually, it doesn't bother me. Families are supposed to wind each other up, aren't they? It never seems to annoy Buff. He's used to it. Today, I'm not in the mood for their winding. I am annoyed on my husband's behalf.

'Leave Buff alone,' I snap. 'He's going slow because of the baby.'

'What?' says Matty.

'There's a baby?' says Cathy.

'Wow, congratulations,' says Clodagh, already two steps ahead of the others.

'I thought we were going to wait 'til everybody was together,' says Buff.

'Sorry, love,' I say, placing my hand over his hand where it's resting on the gear stick. 'It just slipped out.' I turn to face the backseat. 'Yeah,' I say. 'It's early days, but it looks like we're going to have a wee one in January.' I remove my hand from the gear stick and pat my stomach lightly. The motion's already instinctive.

'That's amazing news,' says Clodagh.

'Well done, big lad,' says Matty, squeezing Buff's shoulder. 'I didn't think you had it in you.'

'I'm going to be an auntie,' says Cathy. She tries to hug me from behind, stretching her arms round the passenger seat's headrest, almost throttling me in the process.

Clodagh whips out the Percy Pigs. 'I think this calls for a celebration,' she says, 'Percy Pigs all round.' She passes the packet into the front seat. I turn the music up. 'Rainy Days and Mondays' comes on. It's not a particularly upbeat choice but the only two CD's Buff has in his car are *The Best of the Carpenters* and *The Carpenters Covered*.

I glance over at my husband. He's watching the young ones. He still has an eye on the road. The other's trained on the rear-view mirror. He's holding the steering wheel carefully with both hands. He is smiling. Buff's not given to shows of emotion, but I can tell he's made up right now. We've not discussed how the announcement will play out. We don't want a big fuss. Neither of us enjoy being the centre of attention. Still, it's great to see how excited the backseat contingent are. This baby's a big deal for us. We've been waiting a long time for it. By waiting, I mean trying. By trying, I mean doctors' appointments and schedules, prescriptive sex and four rounds of IVF. We've spent all the money we were saving for the loft conversion, and the conservatory, and the new kitchen. It has been worth it though. The minute those wee lines appeared on the test I knew it had all been worth it.

I won't forget that morning in a hurry. Buff was waiting for me when I came out of the loo. I was still holding the stick. I'd it bundled up in a wad of toilet roll. I tried to tell him it was positive. I was crying so much I couldn't get the words out. Poor Buff, he wasn't sure whether they were good or bad tears. He'd seen me come out of the toilet bawling that many times before. He took the test out of my hand; it was covered in pee but he didn't even bother with the toilet roll. He stared at it for ages, his big face all screwed up in concentration.

Eventually, he looked up at me and said, 'Two lines is good, right?'

I nodded.

'We're having a baby?'

I nodded.

I probably should have said, *We've a long way to go yet, love. Wait 'til we talk to the doctor. It might not work out.* But I knew in the pit of my belly, this one was going to stick. Sometimes you just know a thing is inevitable. There's a heaviness to it. It was like that with me and Buff. The first time I saw him at the bus stop, I just knew that was me forever; stuck with him, in a good way. We were sixteen when we started going out.

We're thirty-four now. It shouldn't have taken so long to get to this point, but nothing's ever come easy to us. Well, nothing except getting together. That felt like falling. We couldn't have avoided each other, even if we'd wanted to.

'I can't believe we're finally having a baby,' Buff said, still holding the test in one hand.

I wrapped my arms around him. He held me differently; sort of gentler, like he was scared of crushing the baby. I'm a good bit shorter than he is, so when I whispered, 'I can't believe it either,' the sentiment was lost. All my words disappeared into his chest, while my ear – angled, as it was, towards his chin – caught everything he said, ('God, I can't wait to tell Mam and Dad'). I wished I hadn't heard for it stung to know that even during this, the most intimate of moments, his parents were still first and foremost in his thoughts. I let it go. I didn't want to ruin the moment. I understood where he was coming from. I've always understood. My parents aren't great either.

Buff's the oldest but he's never been their first or favourite. When he's in one of his moods he'll say, 'They only had me to practice so they could get everything right with Brian.' It's probably not true. It feels like it is. Buff's the screw-up. Brian's the golden boy. For every shit storm we've muddled through – my redundancy, Buff's diabetes, the bungalow subsiding, the baby stuff – Brian's enjoyed unmerited success. He's currently on his sixth promotion. If he keeps progressing at this rate, he'll be CEO before he's forty. He has a big house and a holiday home in Portstewart, a full head of hair and a washboard stomach. He's even managed to bag the only woman in County Antrim who looks like a lingerie model and gets on like a minister's wife. In short, Brian's the kind of son William and Susan actually wanted. They're not bad people. They love Buff too, but it's a different kind of love. It's always angled downwards. With Brian, they're constantly looking up.

The baby will change everything. A grandchild will level the playing field. When we drop our bombshell, we'll be front and centre for a change. I can picture the look on their faces. I can pivot like a TV camera round every single one of my in-laws, framing them for a second in my mind. I know who'll be smiling and who'll look like they're sucking lemons. I can tell you right now how it's going to play out this afternoon. Sure, haven't I pictured this moment a hundred times? Haven't I wanted it for Buff almost as much as I wanted it for myself?

They'll all be sitting about on picnic rugs; everybody splayed out on the sand; everybody except Susan who always insists upon a proper deck chair. She uses her arthritis as an excuse. I suspect she thinks her backside's more refined than everyone else's. She'll be sat there like Lady Muck with the anorak draped over her shoulders, Superman-style. The hood may or may not be up. This will depend upon how imminent she believes the rain to be. She'll be the one who pours the tea and butters the pancakes and, every thirty seconds says, 'Is everybody alright for something?' It is Susan who will decide when it's time for William's birthday cake. She is the matriarch. Her role is long-established. Nobody, not even Clodagh, is brave enough to mount a challenge.

Cathy will light the candles and come at her daddy with whatever's left of the Victoria sponge. This too is set in stone. As the only girl child, it's always been her job to present the birthday cake and start the singing. 'Happy Birthday to you,' she'll begin, and everyone will quickly join in. 'Happy Birthday to you. Happy Birthday dear William/Dad/Mr McKinley,' (under my breath I will substitute *William* for *Granda* and feel the wee hairs on my arms begin to rise in anticipation of the telling).

Once the cake's cut, and everybody's said, 'it's absolutely delicious, Michelle,' and Michelle's made a point of batting their compliments away like persistent bluebottles, Buff will clear his throat awkwardly and maybe get to his feet. Buff is inclined to be overly formal on occasions like this. 'So,' he'll say, 'Victoria and I have a wee bit of news. Another birthday present, so to speak. There's no other way to say it Dad, but you're going to be a Granda soon.' They'll all smile and ask questions and want to hug us. It will be like how it is when the fans rush on to the pitch after a football match and lift the winning team up in the air, chanting. In my head, it will be exactly like this when we tell them.

It is not like this at all.

Somewhere between the Ballymoney roundabout and Ballybogey it begins to rain.

Susan is miles ahead, bundled up in the backseat of Brian's car, yet I can still hear her pointing out the obvious. 'See,' she'll be saying, barely able to suppress her own smugness, 'I told youse it was for raining. We'll not be able to picnic now.' She'll be enjoying this in her own dour way.

In our car, it is Cathy who notices the rain first.

'Shite,' she says, 'Mam was right. It is for raining.'

Buff switches the wipers on at the lowest setting. The rain smears across the windscreen in dense, spit-thick streaks. It's really only drizzling.

We are optimistic in our car. We have reason for optimism today.

'It's just mizzling,' I say.

'It'll pass,' says Cathy.

'Sure, we've all got coats with us,' says Clodagh.

'It's not as dull looking over there,' says Buff. He inclines his head towards the coast. 'See, that wee patch of blue. That's where we're heading.'

In the back seat, behind Buff, Matty's phone goes off. His ringtone is a fella with a thick Belfast accent yelling, *yeeeeooooww*, stretching the word out so it sounds like some kind of animal noise. He got it off one of the lads in the Rugby Club. It's really annoying. We're on the third *yeeeeooooww* before he manages to fumble the phone out of his pocket and press it to his ear.

'Uh huh,' he says, flapping his hand about to indicate, I'm to turn The Carpenters down. 'It's not too bad here, Shelly. Just drizzling really. Uh huh. She does. Alright then, if Mum thinks it's best. We'll be there in five. Naw, make that ten. Buff's driving.'

He hangs up and slips his phone back into his pocket. 'Michelle says it's lashing at the White Rocks,' he says. 'Absolutely pissing.'

'Will we go somewhere for a coffee instead?' asks Clodagh.

'Aye,' says Cathy. 'There's a nice new place on the Prom in Portstewart.'

'That's far too sensible for the McKinley's,' says Matty. 'Mum says we're not for wasting all the food she's prepared. We'll have the picnic in the car.'

'Seriously?' says Cathy. 'We're not weans anymore. There's hardly any room in here.'

Matty shrugs. 'Mother's spoken. We're having a car picnic. And damn it, Catherine,' he adds, mimicking Susan's dour drawl, 'you'll enjoy every second of it.'

Everyone laughs, even Cathy. 'Remember the time we went to Ayr on the ferry and we ended up having a picnic in the layby next to the sewage plant?'

'How could I forget a magic moment like that?' says Matty.

'You pair are probably too wee to remember,' says Buff, addressing them in the rear-view mirror, 'but Dad once took us all to North Wales for a holiday and it rained the entire time. You wouldn't believe how many picnics we had in the car that week. Youse two always got put in the boot to make room for the rest of us. It was different back then. You could put your children in the boot if you'd a big enough car.'

'Am I wrong here Buff, or did we once have a picnic in a multi-storey car park?' asks Cathy.

'We did indeed, Catherine. That would've been in Conway, on our way to the castle.'

'And, am I completely mad in thinking that Mum set the deck chairs out down the side of the car?'

'No, you are spot on there, Catherine: deckchairs, icebox, china cups for the tea. Our mother knows how to picnic properly, even when she's serving sandwiches out the back of a clapped-out Astra.'

Clodagh has been noticeably silent throughout this exchange. I can see her wee face in the mirror. She looks perplexed.

'Is it a Protestant thing?' she asks. 'Having your picnic in the car? 'Cause it's not something my folks do.'

'Naw,' says Cathy quickly.

'I don't know,' I say. 'Maybe.'

'Absolutely,' says Matty. 'Nobody actually enjoys a car picnic. It's just something you have to endure. Must be a Protestant thing.'

Everyone laughs except Buff. He turns to look at me. I can tell exactly what's bothering him. His face is like a window. I can see right through him.

'Don't worry,' I say. 'It'll be grand. We can still tell them. We'll just wait for the right moment.'

'But it won't be like we planned it.'

'It'll be grand,' I repeat. I pat Buff's thigh. I smile, reassuringly. 'Sure, it doesn't matter how we tell them.'

He doesn't look convinced.

'Your folks are going to be over the moon,' I say.

He nods a little. He's about to let himself smile.

'And even if they're not as excited as we want them to be, sure, it doesn't matter, Buff. It's our baby. Who cares what they think?'

The instant the words are out of my mouth, I can tell I've said the wrong thing. Buff's mouth sets. His hands grip the steering wheel so tightly I can see the white of bones knuckling through his skin.

'I care what they think,' he says. His voice is raw as ripped paper. He's practically shouting. The backseat contingent have definitely heard. The air is heavier inside the car now. It takes ten minutes to drive to the White Rocks and nobody attempts to break the silence. When we arrive in the car park, Buff pulls up next to Brian's Audi.

Michelle's standing beside the open boot, an umbrella clutched in one hand, in the other, a Tupperware full of white bread sandwiches. She's chatting to Susan. The boot has swallowed her head and torso. The only part of my mother-in-law that's visible is her backside, bent and straining beneath the confines of that godawful skirt. I can't see what she's doing in there: filling teacups no doubt, or slicing up wheaten, creaming individual meringues for dessert.

They've started without us. Behind the fogged-up windows of the Audi I can see Brian tucking into what might be a chocolate éclair. William has a mug in his hand. I can't see for condensation but I'd be reasonably certain it's his favourite John Deere one. He won't take his tea in anything else. The women are seeing to the men before they eat themselves.

'I'll go and give them a hand,' I say.

It's not so much duty as habit. Buff does nothing to stop me. He'll expect me to bring the tea to his door. It doesn't matter if I get drenched in the process. Tea making's a woman's job here. I don't resent the assumption. He knows better. It's not how we are, together, in our own wee house. But here there's his father to consider and his brothers too. I wouldn't want him losing face in front of them. As soon as the motor's stopped I open the front door. Michelle was right. It is absolutely lashing. I open the glove compartment and remove my umbrella. I stick it out the door and force it open before I slide out.

'Do you want some help?' asks Clodagh.

'Naw,' I say, 'no point in us both getting soaked. I'll bring the food over to youse.'

I give Cathy a bit of a look. Clodagh's a guest. I wouldn't expect her to help. But Cathy's one of us. She should've offered at least. I close the passenger door and pick my way through the puddles to the back of Brian's Audi.

'Sorry, we took so long,' I say.

Michelle gives me a watery smile. 'We started without you,' she says. She isn't apologising. She's merely stating a fact. 'Do you want a sandwich?' she asks, extending the Tupperware box. 'There's paper plates in the boot.'

'Aye, I'll take some over to the ones in our car.'

I take the Tupperware from Michelle and go into the boot for the plates. It is immediately apparent that Susan has not heard us arrive. You can hear almost nothing with your head ducked under the parcel shelf. She starts when she sees my face come looming towards her. She almost drops the mug she's filling. It's a fine bone china number with a pheasant printed on the side. A wee slurp of hot tea goes slopping over its edge, lands in the open sugar bowl and forms a brown crystalized lump. Susan clearly hasn't noticed, or she'd be in there picking it out with a teaspoon.

'Goodness, Victoria,' she says, straightening up, 'where did you appear from?'

'We just arrived,' I say. 'I'm after some plates.' I switch hands in order to hold my umbrella over Susan's head. My own hair's getting wet now, but I don't want my mother-in-law adding thoughtlessness to my ever-growing list of faults.

'They're in there, next to the cool box,' she says. She makes no effort to assist me.

'Right. Thanks.' I reach in, straining to make sure Susan's still protected by my umbrella. I lift out a wad of paper plates. 'It's a pity about the rain.'

'I told youse it was going to rain. We might've missed it, if we'd left earlier.'

'Uch well,' I say, 'we'll not let a bit of rain ruin the afternoon. We've a lot to celebrate.'

'We do indeed,' says Susan, her whole face lights up. She's like the inside of a fridge when the door opens; sort of glowy. She smiles over my shoulder at Michelle. Though I can't see her, I can feel Michelle smiling back. I wonder if she knows. Maybe Buff's told Brian, and Brian's told Michelle, and Michelle's told Susan. It'd be just like Michelle to tell Susan. Michelle's way more calculating than she lets on.

'What do you mean?' I ask tentatively. 'William's birthday?'

'Aye, well of course there's William's birthday to celebrate,' says Susan. 'But there's the baby too. I've only just heard.'

'You have.'

'Aye, I suppose I'm probably the last to know.'

I shrug. I'm not sure who knows and who doesn't know anymore. Over Susan's shoulder I watch Matty draw a sad face in the condensation. They're probably starving in there. Any second now they'll wind the windows down and start baying for sandwiches.

'How did you find out?' I ask.

'It was my fault,' interrupts Michelle. 'I let it slip.'

Bitch, I think. I manage to keep this thought to myself. Later tonight, when we're on our own, I'll have a good old moan to Buff. He doesn't mind me giving off about his sister-in-law though he never joins in himself.

Susan slips an arm round Michelle's almost non-existent waist. 'I'm glad you told us, sweetheart,' she says.

'I thought you should know. Brian said I shouldn't tell you but it's a big deal – your first grand-baby – I thought you should know straight away, Susan.'

'It's so funny the way it came out,' Susan says, smiling. 'Wait 'til you hear what happened,

Victoria. The pair of us were in the boot here, getting things sorted and I said to Michelle, Michelle you have to try one of these cream cheese and grape sandwiches. I got the idea for them from *Bella* magazine. They're absolutely gorgeous. Then Michelle says to me, I can't eat cream cheese at the minute Susan, because of the baby. And, well, that's how it slipped out, Victoria. Isn't that hilarious?'

I nod dumbly. My head feels far too heavy for my neck. If I wasn't holding the stupid umbrella over Susan, I'd have my hands under my chin, taking the weight of it off my neck.

Susan mistakes my silence for interest. 'She's not that far gone, are you Michelle?'

'Only eight weeks, Susan. It's early days.'

In my head I am thinking eight weeks is far too early to be telling folks. I've lost babies at nine weeks and eleven. I wouldn't go shouting about an eight-week baby. It's far too soon. It might not last.

'I'm glad you've told us,' Susan continues, pouring the tea as she talks. 'I mean you wouldn't want to be telling everyone at this stage. But family's different, isn't it Victoria?'

'Yes,' I say. 'Family's different.'

I look over at our car. Buff's wiped a hole in the condensation. He's peering out of it, his mouth hung open like a fish. He has a particularly gormless look off him when he's hungry. My poor husband, I think. He doesn't know yet. He's sat there waiting for me to bring him a ham sandwich and after that, a slice of buttered wheaten, and he is genuinely happy in himself; more happy than he's been in years. He still thinks the day is going to be ours.

I am overcome with feelings for my husband. There's a bit of love in there and a lot of pity and a thing which I believe to be righteous anger. I pull the umbrella away from Susan's head and cover my own. I purposefully angle the umbrella's edge so a big plop of water drips off and runs down the back of her neck. It is no real consolation, but I can't say it doesn't give me a little rush of pleasure to see Susan start and whack her head off the parcel shelf, sloshing hot coffee over her cardigan sleeve.

'Whoops,' I say. I stop myself from apologising. 'I'm just going to take Buff his tea. Congratulations Michelle. I'm delighted for you and Brian.' I say this last part in the same voice I use for offering the bereaved sympathy after a funeral. I am steady. I am serious. I am, perhaps, a little too sombre.

I take Buff's tea over to him. I lean through the open window to offer him his choice of sandwiches. I can see they've already been picked over. Brian and William have lifted all the chicken ones. I watch him make his selection, choosing the best of the leftovers. It's not like me at all, but I'm suddenly struck with the need to kiss him, right there, in front of everyone. It's not something we usually do. Neither is it desire. It is simply meeting a need. I take his big head in my hands. I kiss him lightly on the lips and I call him by his real name. 'William,' I say, 'you are the best.' This will mean more to him than saying *I love you*, or *I'm proud of you*, or any of that sappy shite. It's first place Buff's after. God love him, he's only ever been second.

We'll not tell the in-laws today. The moment's gone.

When the rain eases off, we'll circle round Brian's car with the rest of them: the young men standing, Susan and William on the deckchairs, us girls resting up against the open boot, our backsides competing for space. When the birthday cake candles are blown out and Brian says he has something to tell us I'll walk over to my husband's side. I'll take his hand and squeeze it tightly. I'll not have to say anything. He'll know, as I know, not to mention our baby. Today is Brian and Michelle's day. We can't take away from their news.

We'll congratulate the pair of them. We will measure our words carefully, saying enough to cover ourselves but no more. We'll accept a slice of Victoria sponge on a clean paper plate and eat without pleasure. Two bites in, I'll assure Michelle that the cake's absolutely grand, that the heat's not got to it at all. Between the nine of us, we'll devour the whole thing. Then, noticing the way the men are scraping at their plates, I will say, 'There's a wee Marks and Spencer's coffee cake in there. I could open it if youse are still hungry.'

Susan will look at me like I've two heads, and say, 'We don't need another cake, Victoria. Don't be opening it. Take it home with youse and put it in the freezer.'

I'll say, 'I brought it for William, for his birthday. Why don't youse take it home with you?'

'William doesn't like coffee cake,' she'll say.

I will be overcome by the desire to stab her with my disposable, plastic cake fork. I will be able to feel the press of it jabbing into her throat, right beneath her hairy chin. I will picture the red blood dripping unto her pale pink anorak; the stains it'll leave on that pastel skirt. My mouth will be full of vicious words; things I've always wanted to say to her. Buff will squeeze my hand then, just a little squeeze: a reminder rather than a restraint.

'I could go for a bit of coffee cake,' he'll say. 'What about yourself, Matty? Hoke it out of the cool bag there, Vicky.'

I will understand then that Buff has been holding me all this time; ages and ages, in his own gentle way. I am holding Buff too. I have been holding him tight – so tight and close – since the first moment I clapped eyes on him, standing there, next to the bus stop in his too-small school uniform. I have wanted to hold on to this man. I have wanted him to hold on to me. We may well be holding on by the skin of our teeth but neither one of us has any notion of letting go.

The Grotesques

Sarah Hall

IF SHE'D BEEN SOMEONE else, the prank might have seemed funny. The vagrant Charlie-bo, who was quite famous around town, a kind of filthy savant, was lying on his back in his usual spot under the shop awning. He was asleep or passed out. Perhaps he was even dead, Dilly couldn't tell. A mask of fruit and vegetables had been arranged over his face to create another awful face. Lemons for eyes – the pupils drawn in black marker pen. A leering banana smile. Corncobs were stacked round his head as a spray of wild hair. The nose – how had they done it? – was an upright slice of melon, carved, balanced, its orange flesh drying and dulling. It was all horribly artistic. Dilly stood close by, staring. The face was monstrous and absurd, like one of the paintings in the Fitzwilliam. There was a makeshift palette of newspaper under Charlie-bo, and his feet and hands were upturned and huge. He wore as many layers as a cabbage, and over the holey, furling garments, that enormous grey gown, a cross between a greatcoat and a prophet's robe, tied with a pleated cord.

Dilly hadn't meant to stop; she was late getting home with Mummy's shopping. But the scene was too terrible. People were walking past, bustling around her. Some were making unkind comments. *Good God, look at the state.* There had even been a few laughs, and some clapping, as if this were a street performance. It might have been art, but Charlie-bo hadn't done this to himself; Dilly knew that. He was so far gone, a wreck of a man, a joke already. He lumbered around town and could barely speak. Often he was prostrate in a doorway, drunk. The prank must have been carried out in daylight – brazenly. She could hear an internal voice, Mummy's voice: *Disgraceful, who are these wretches?*

Students, that was who. They were back after the summer break, spoiled from Mediterranean sailing and expensive capital apartments, or loafing on their estates, whatever they did. There had been several esoteric japes in the city since their return. A Halloween mask and nipple-peep bra had been placed over one of the stone saints outside St Giles. The Corpus Clock had been defaced, its glass shield painted with an obscene image, so the rocking brass insect looked like it was performing a sexual act – having a sexual act performed on it, actually. Edward had seen and reported back to Mummy, who was outraged and still talking about it, even though she had no association with the college, or any of the colleges. Edward had seemed rather amused, but quickly sobered in solidarity. First-term antics. Once the Gowns arrived back, they imperiously reclaimed the town, before settling in and getting on with their studies.

Poor Charlie-bo. It was really too much. He wasn't a statue on a church. Dilly wanted to kneel down and remove the ridiculous fruit, shake him awake, help him to his feet. Perhaps if she did, Charlie-bo would revert to his old self, smile and speak articulately, as he hadn't for years. He would thank her. Those reddened, free-roaming eyes would hold her gaze, kindly, shyly. Something spiritual would pass, perhaps – a blessing story, like those Father Muturi had preached about last Sunday. Dilly lifted her hand, paused. The lemon pupils were looking right at her. Charlie-bo's coat was grimy, lined by the dirty tides of the street, and there was a strong, crotchy smell. *Silly girl,* she heard Mummy say. *Don't be so squeamish.*

Mummy was right, of course. She usually was. She could immediately detect faults, like recoil and embarrassment, in her children, even if she couldn't find her own purse or shoe, or she'd lost the car, or a bit of bacon grease was in her hair, making it rear up. Dilly sometimes thought that Mummy was like a truffle pig, rooting around and unearthing ugly, tangled thoughts in people. She especially did not like shame or reticence. You had to stride into a room; wear any dress, day or night, like you were at a gala event; speak to strangers without inhibition. *Just have a go, Dilly, for goodness' sake. Engage!* By now, Mummy would have swept the degrading parody face away and helped stand Charlie-bo up, with that superhuman little woman's strength of hers. Even if he were dead, she would have the power to resurrect him. She would buy him a cup of tea in Jarrold's. Then she'd tell the story, marvellously, afterwards.

Dilly put her hand back in her pocket. Without warning, Charlie-bo flinched. He jolted, as if struck by an electrical current. The melon tipped over, and a lemon rolled from his eye socket on to the pavement, quite near Dilly's foot. Charlie-bo grunted, reached up and groped at his head. He looked like someone on the television coming round from an operation, trying to remove tubes. The banana and corncobs fell away and the real face was revealed: discoloured skin with reefs of eczema and cold-burns, a sore, sticky mouth.

Charlie-bo kept patting his head, making panicked, bleating noises. His eyes – Dilly hadn't been this close to him before – were a mad yellowish-green. There were watery cysts in his eyelids. His gaze was trying to find purchase on something. The striped awning. Sky. Her. He sat up. He flailed an arm out, brushed Dilly's skirt, and blurted a sound that seemed fatty and accusing. Dilly took a step backwards. She shook her head. *No,* she thought. *I wanted to help.* Charlie-bo was looking at her, and through her. He made another attempt to speak. His tongue was oversized, a giant grub inside his mouth. She took another step backwards, and a cyclist tinged his bell in warning and flew past. Someone bumped her hard on her thigh with the corner of a shopping bag. Dilly turned and began to walk away.

Behind her, she could hear Charlie-bo making loud, obscene noises. She sped up, weaving round pedestrians. He might be up on his feet now, lumbering after her. *It wasn't me,* she thought. *Please please please.* She half-ran towards the punt station and Queen's Bridge, her heart flurrying. She passed Lillian's boutique. The door was open and she thought someone said her name, but she kept her head down. Before she turned the corner by the wine merchant, she cast a look behind, expecting to see him, his cloak flying, his face hideous with rage. But Charlie-bo wasn't there. She came to a stop by the river, feeling woozy with relief.

The towpath was quiet, just a few people walking and cycling. She went a little way along and sat on a bench, waited for her nerves to calm. The river was a rich opaque green. Leaves from the chestnut trees had fallen and were riding along on the surface. The river always made her feel better. It would be lovely to walk that way home, the long way round, watch the swans and the glassy fluid sliding over the weir. But she was probably very late now and Mummy would be getting cross. Mummy had only sent Dilly out for a few items – teabags, cream, jam. It had taken a long time to decide on the jam. Dilly couldn't remember if Mummy had asked for a particular kind, and she'd begun to fixate on the seeds in the raspberry jam jar. They'd seemed like a million prickly eyes.

People were coming over to the house for a little get-together that afternoon – it was Dilly's birthday, actually, though the fact kept slipping her mind. Father Muturi, who was Mummy's favourite priest at St Eligius, was coming, and Cleo and

Dominic, of course, possibly Peter if he finished work in time, not Rebecca, obviously, though Dilly still sometimes forgot, and a lady was coming who could perhaps help Dilly get a job at a magazine, on the arts column. Dilly had wanted to ask Sam, but it was beginning to look like Sam didn't meet with anyone's approval. He'd been a bit too quiet at the dinner last week, and hadn't wanted to sing when Mummy had asked him to. When Dilly had sung her number, a northern sea shanty, which she'd performed nicely but with the usual mild mortification, Sam had looked suddenly very frightened. He hadn't replied to Dilly's last three messages. And he hadn't been to their French evening class this week.

Mummy was making scones for the tea party, which was quite a production; things would be getting tense at home, even though scones, as far as Dilly could tell, were not very difficult to make. She should really go. *Get on, Dilly!* She should be thinking of interesting things to say to the lady from the arts magazine, and sorting her face out. But the river was so smooth and lovely. It felt very receptive. She'd walked along it with Rebecca in the summer, on a very hot day, and had tried to say kind things. She'd said that, as Peter's little sister, she knew him as well as anyone did, and, even if he seemed a bit *other*, she was sure he did care. It wasn't a disloyal thing to say, she'd hoped. Rebecca had been crying on the walk, silently, her face was soaked, her unwashed hair pulled back under a headband, and she hadn't replied. Rebecca had cried a lot last summer, because of the baby. And because of Peter, though Mummy maintained Peter had done nothing wrong, that he couldn't take leave from work willy-nilly, and that Rebecca had been crying to *a worrying degree* and might be becoming *a rather difficult character*. It was hard to know what to think about it. Or feel about it. Dilly had written a few letters to Rebecca, but had thrown them away. It couldn't be spoken about, unless raised by Mummy, and then certain agreements were made.

A good party story to tell would have been how she'd helped Charlie-bo, how she'd intervened, stopped the ridicule. It was so hard to make yourself the hero of your stories, be witty but still seem humble – Mummy and Cleo were masters at that kind of thing.

Dilly looked downstream. It was the usual scene. Houseboats with bicycles mounted on their sides. Joggers. The metal bridge – Sorrell's – the only ugly bridge in the city. There were some newly built houses with chalet-style balconies that Edward liked. Who lived there, she wondered. Different people. The common opened out, and the river trickled away to nothing on the horizon.

She became aware of a light rain falling. Her skirt was damp and the towpath now had a leaden sheen. The swans were tucked away, heads under their wings, holding so still in the current they could be pegged underwater. She'd forgotten to take an umbrella from the house, of course. Her hair was difficult if the rain got it for too long, *unmanageable,* which would be a problem later. She stood and began to walk back towards the punt station. The drops were already getting heavy; she could feel them trickling on her forehead and round her eyebrows. The punts were parked in a row, hooded and chained. Four or five people were looking over the edge on the bank opposite, up above the weir. One person was pointing. Something was probably caught in the froth at the bottom of the water's curtain. It was one of Mummy's peeves, all the junk being tossed into the river — riparian fly-tipping, she called it. Suitcases, bin bags, toasters. Almost as bad as the uncleared dog mess and barbecue scorches on The Green.

Dilly didn't have time to stop and look. She turned, walked over Queen's Bridge and continued up the road, past the charity shop, which always had lovely blouses on its mannequins, past The Blue Bell, towards Monns Patisserie. Monns was very difficult. There was a kind of pastel, underworld glory to the window. The cakes were tormentingly delicious, with such delicate architecture and sugar-spun geometrics, candied fruit, chocolate curls. She often found herself gazing at them and getting lost. It was best not even to look. But she couldn't help it. Today, the cakes seemed so perfect and beautiful that she began to feel emotional. Her throat hurt. She wanted to sit down on the pavement and hold her knees.

She was hungry; that was it. An egg for breakfast was all Mummy had allowed, no toast because Dilly was currently off carbs. Lunch hadn't seemed to materialise. Instead, there'd been a little debate about what to wear to impress the lady from the magazine. Several skirts were rejected, and there had been a lot of frustration in the room. Mummy and the lady, her name was possibly Marion or Beatrice, had fallen out a few years ago over something written in an article. Now they were friends again. That was not uncommon with Mummy's acquaintances.

One of the cakes in Monns seemed to have a waterfall of glittering cocoa powder on its edge, almost hovering, suspended in the air. How had they done that? Perhaps her eyes were blurring in the rain. *Do buck up, Dilly.* Soon there would be scones, Mummy's speciality: warm, soft, comforting, with cream and jam. It might be possible to slip an extra one on to her plate unseen. There was an art to second helpings: you had to be confident and move fast, look as if you were helpfully clearing crockery. Dilly wondered if Charlie-bo was hungry. There was the question of alcohol, which might take priority. Of all the homeless people in town, Charlie-bo was best known, cherished even. He'd been a student at the university, studying Heidegger, or the eleventh dynamic of space, something very avant-garde and awfully difficult. He'd been in contention for a Nobel, people said. Mummy maintained Charlie-bo was from a small northern village, just like her – an unbelonger, a bootstrapping scholarship boy. Too much studying, or a drug trauma, or a stroke – some calamity had done for him, and he'd begun his descent. For a while he'd been a brilliant celebrity of the streets and shelters, until his mind dissolved. A casualty of genius. At least, that was the story.

By the time she got to Northumberland Road, Dilly felt wet and dizzy. The rain had done a very thorough job. Her hair stuck to her temples. The bottom door of the house was locked – its key had been missing for a while – which meant she wouldn't be able to slip in unnoticed. She trudged up the steps to the front door and through the window saw Father Muturi in the lounge, standing at the fireplace and talking to Edward. Father Muturi liked to stand by the fire and say how cold England was. He would say things like African children learned to walk younger because it was warmer there.

If Edward had been called down, Dilly was very late. She waited outside for a moment, very close to the front door, perhaps only an inch from it. She could feel her breath against the wood. The smell from her mouth was like pickle. She could see cracks in the red paint. Inside one was the tiniest insect – its legs poking out, awkwardly. She put her hand on the knob. She took it off again. Sometimes doors could seem impossible. Impossible to open. Impossible to walk through. She felt as if she was the door, as if her own body was shut. Her hair was wet and stupid. Her coat was dripping. *Lordy! Have you been for a dip at the river club, Dilly?* She could hear cars on the street, the squealing brakes of a bicycle as it slowed at the bottom of the hill.

Recently, Mummy had arranged a session with Merrick, the psychoanalyst who lived at number 52, to talk about things like this, and give Dilly 'a bit of a boost'. *You can tell me anything you like,* Merrick had said. *Anything about anything.* It had seemed almost like a riddle, the way he'd said that. *Should we start with why you came back from London?* Merrick had been wearing terrible socks with orange diamonds on the ankles, perhaps in an ironic way. It was strange seeing him away from Mummy's parties, where he was usually dancing, or flirting with Cleo. His practice was in the basement of his own house, and Dilly could see the shoes and legs of people walking past on the street above. She even saw the red-tipped, winking underparts of a dog. The furniture wasn't leather; it was suede, mustard colour. There was a painting on the wall that was abstract but looked like a woman with a whirlpool in her stomach. Was it supposed to look that way, Dilly had wondered, or did it look like different things to different people? Was it, in fact, a kind of test?

Dilly had prepared things to say to Merrick, all very carefully thought through, but she hadn't said much in the end. *After my bag was stolen, I didn't feel very safe in London.* The truth was, no single cataclysmic incident had occurred. It was more a series of daily stumbles, problems she couldn't solve alone. The forgetting of meals, not forgetting exactly but being defeated by so many options, and rent payments, not making the milk convert to perfect, solid foam in the cafe where she worked. Merrick had looked rather sceptical and bored for most of the hour, then, towards the end, disappointed. He'd finished the session with a little talk about boundaries and identity within a family, he'd used a fishing-net metaphor, and Dilly had felt uncomfortable and was glad when it was over. Mummy hadn't asked her about the session.

The rain was coming down, pattering, darkening the pavement. She would be spied any moment, by Edward or Father Muturi. The scones couldn't be served until the jam and cream, which were in the bottom of Dilly's bag, had been delivered. Mummy liked Dilly to make up the tea tray for guests, using the Minton set. Dilly couldn't exactly explain her lateness; she never could. It was, it would be, more a question of absorbing the annoyance. Letting Mummy's words come into her without feeling them. One possibility was to tell the Charlie-bo story; somehow amend it and seem less uninvolved. If she told it interestingly, earnestly, with the beautiful sneer and radio tone of Cleo, or with something approximating Mummy's comedic affront, that might be good enough. She might hold the room. She would, of course, be asked about her level of activity. *Didn't you do anything, Dilly, for goodness' sake?* Perhaps she could say she had done something. Mummy would. Mummy could change a story or revise history with astonishing audacity, and seemed to instantly believe the new version.

Edward was waving at her through the window, mouthing *door's unlocked,* which of course it always was, even when they all went off on holiday. She pushed it and stepped into the hallway. There were voices in the lounge, Edward's affable small talk, and Father Muturi's lovely Kenyan laugh. *I just need to take these,* she called. She heeled off her boots and went very quietly downstairs to the kitchen. Ghost steps: she was an expert. From the kitchen came the gorgeous, golden smell of baking. The table was in chaos, bowls of spilling flour and dribbling eggshells, some lilies still wrapped in plastic dumped in a jug. The tea tray was not set up. Mummy was turned away, bent over the open oven. There was a white handprint of flour on her skirt. She had on fishnet tights and heels, which meant Dilly would have to find a pair of heels too.

The scone smell was almost unbearable. She was so hungry. If she could have just an apple before trying to make polite conversation with the lady from the arts magazine, things might be

OK. But the fruit bowl was empty except for a glove. Mummy was naturally slight and trim. Her children were all taller and heavier, like their father with *broad Dutch genes,* and their intake had to be watched. Daughters, anyway. Peter and Dominic were allowed to finish the roast when they were home, then play tennis afterwards to work it off, while the girls cleared up.

The oven fan was whirring. Classical music was playing on the stereo. Mummy hadn't noticed Dilly; she was busy flapping the scones with a tea towel. Her hair was spilling from its blonde nest. Dilly put her bag quietly down on the table, removed the jam and cream. She placed them behind the flower jug, where it might seem they'd been sitting innocently for an hour, then backed out of the kitchen. She ran upstairs, past the hall mirror – yes, she looked a mess, mascara smudged, lips pale, drowned-cat hair – up to the second floor and into the bathroom. She shut the door, moved the linen basket in front of it. She looked in the bathroom cabinet for a volumiser, some kind of lacquering spray. There was a box of half-used hair dye, magazine sample sachets of face cream, Edward's cologne and an old splayed toothbrush. Nothing helpful.

Below, the doorbell rang. More party guests arriving, probably, though there were always people coming and going for other reasons. She half-expected to hear Mummy's voice calling up – *Door, Dill-eee* – as if Mummy might sense, might even see, somehow, that she was home. Dilly picked a towel up off the floor, sat on the toilet lid, and rubbed her hair. There was a comb in the bathtub and she scraped it through her fringe, tried to create something chic to one side of her head. She was sure she had a nice lipstick somewhere, a dark, sophisticated red, given to her by Cleo, who was always being sent free cosmetics. It had come in a little metallic sack, and was called something strange that didn't suggest colour at all, but a mood, a state of fortune. *Advantage. Ascent.* She sat for a while thinking, but couldn't remember the name.

The lounge was extremely warm when Dilly went in. A furnace of coal glowed in the fire's cradle. There was simmering laughter and conversation, the gentle clanking of cups on saucers. Everyone had arrived: Cleo, Dominic and his wife, Bella, Peter, who was in his officer's uniform, the magazine lady, or at least an unknown lady in a black dress, and some of Mummy's other friends. Dilly tried to enter the room with a combination of subtle grace and moderate drama, to be seen and perhaps admired, but also pass into the throng without much notice or comment. Mummy was beside the table pouring tea into cups on saucers held out by Bella. Bella was very good at helping, and she seemed to have doubled her efforts since Rebecca. Mummy had on a little blonde fur stole and a black cardigan. There was still a faint white flour mark on her skirt. Next to the tea tray sat a plate of perfect, mounded, bronzed scones. The jam and cream had evidently been found and were set out in matching bowls. Dilly was desperate for a scone, but Mummy was right there, so she moved towards Edward, who, more often than not, would give up his plate if he saw a lady without.

As she was making her way round the perimeter of the group, Cleo turned and took hold of Dilly's elbow. *If it isn't the mystery birthday girl,* she said. *What have you been up to? Spying for the government?* She kissed Dilly on the cheek. Cleo smelled heavenly, some kind of antique French talcum, or a salon-grade shampoo. Her hair, tresses and tresses of it, was piled high. She had on a silky maroon item, not a dress, nor a jumper; it draped perfectly from her shoulders and was belted at her waist. Her face was dewy, flawless. *Goodness, you do look beautiful, Dilly, what a fabulous combination, very laissez-faire.* Dilly had

put together long, wide suit trousers on loan from
Lillian's shop, part of the new winter range, and a
pink silk shirt rifled from Edward's cupboard. In
her haste to get ready, the combination had
seemed a stroke of casual sartorial humour. But
when Cleo gave compliments, you could never
quite be sure whether there wasn't another
message. Cleo lowered her voice, conspiratorially.
Just a moment, there's a tiny bit. She raised her top
lip and pointed to her front teeth. Cleo's teeth
were slightly gapped, making her somehow seem
both sexual and childlike. Dilly licked around to
remove the lipstick. *Thanks.* Cleo tutted. *Bit of a
dull crew this afternoon, isn't it?* Her mouth rode
upwards. She looked like the most beautiful
snarling show dog. *Shame Sam couldn't come. But
probably it's not his kind of thing? Let's say hi to the
boys.*

Cleo linked her arm through Dilly's and
stepped her towards their brothers. Peter and
Dominic kissed Dilly on both cheeks and resumed
their conversation, which sounded political,
something to do with a war in Venezuela. They
were disagreeing, amiably. Cleo began a funny
anecdote – inserting it elegantly into the discussion
– about when she had flown to the wrong airport
in Venezuela, the plane landing in a field full of
little horses, and getting a lift to Barquisimeto

with some chaps who it turned out were not really all that savoury. Peter laughed quietly, uncontrollably; Cleo knew exactly her audience. Dominic looked as if he was gearing up for a story of his own, but he probably knew it wouldn't compete.

The four Quinn siblings, standing together in a group. For a few nice moments, it felt to Dilly like a completed puzzle. It hadn't felt that way for a while, not since things with Rebecca, which Mummy described as *one of the worst things to have happened to the family,* her attachment, her over-attachment, to the baby. Some of the words that had been said, by Rebecca when she was very upset, and also by Mummy, afterwards, had echoed in Dilly's head a long time. *Congenital. Abusive. Your son's twisted priorities and your bloody eugenics – now it's fine to destroy life?* Dilly didn't know how people could believe in exact opposites where humans were concerned. Mummy could be quite fierce about her sons, but sometimes Peter did need their help, actually, where emotions were concerned. It was awful when things, when people, went wrong. It hadn't really happened since their father had left, and that had been Mummy's predominant brown study, until Rebecca. The greatest betrayal of all was to disaffiliate.

Dilly's tummy hurt. There was a sound in her ears that happened when hunger got to a certain stage, a kind of humming generator noise. She could hear Mummy talking loudly, saying something about *that naughty Peter not being in a proper jacket,* though Mummy quite liked it when Peter arrived at Northumberland Road off-duty, in his kit. Dilly kept her eyes busy and away from the zone where their gazes might meet. In a moment Mummy would probably come over, say something remonstrative, and want to introduce Dilly to the magazine lady. There would be one of those rapid, awkward, whispery interrogations about where Dilly had been, *mousing off again,* and then she'd have to pretend to be poised and ready for an interview, which wasn't a proper interview, but a kind of cultural conversation test that might lead to some work, or at the very least to a temporary internship that might lead to some work. Dilly had read the arts section of the papers at the weekend, but couldn't remember anything interesting. She had half an idea for an article about the colour yellow, how yellow was being reclaimed by women after years of being unfashionable. Also colour therapy, how yellow had a certain effect, psychologically, in relation to mental health. Dilly hadn't quite worked the proposition out yet, but if she started talking, hopefully things would expand. The room was stuffy and a bit smoky and she felt sick. It was a dangerous point; she knew that from the past. She really did have to eat.

She slid out of Cleo's arm, and went over to Edward and Father Muturi. Father Muturi seemed not to have moved an inch from his warm spot. *Cleo,* he exclaimed, *I was hoping to meet you! Actually, I'm Dilly,* Dilly said, *that's Cleo there.* She pointed. There was a pause. *Ah yes, Delia.* Father Muturi turned to Edward. *She comes to church a lot, this one. A good girl. Yes, I know,* said Edward. *That's a splendid shirt, Dilly. I was thinking of wearing it myself.* Edward was smiling, eyes pale and bright behind his glasses. His face was purplish-red, which made his hair look extraordinarily white. He must be cooking inside his wool cardigan. It had taken a little while, but Edward had got used to the borrowing arrangements in the house. Only his brown Belstaff was off-limits. It was very expensive, his favourite coat, and couldn't be risked, especially as the boys were known to misplace coats a lot. Mummy sometimes teased Edward about it, called it *his lucky war correspondent's jacket,* but they seemed to have reached an agreement.

Father Muturi's plate was empty on the

mantleshelf, but Edward still had half a scone, the bottom piece cut very cleanly, with no scattered crumbs. He hadn't yet spread anything on top. Dilly willed him to see – to feel – how desperate she was. But Edward seemed slower than usual, or less observant, or perhaps he just assumed Dilly had eaten. Father Muturi was coming to the end of his rotation at St Eligius; he was talking about going home. It would be good to get back to those who really needed him. The English were good citizens, not believers. *Well, we shall be very sad to lose you,* Edward was saying, though Edward in fact did not attend Mass unless it was Christmas Eve and he'd had a few vodkas. The skin on his face looked so red and shiny it might burst. As she listened to them talk, everything felt very light and thin, and Dilly thought how kind it would be to reach up and prick the surface of Edward's skin with a pin. Once, twice, on each cheek.

There was a pause in the conversation. *It's my birthday,* Dilly said. *Today. It's today.* The men looked a bit startled. She had blurted it, really quite rudely. *Today?* Father Muturi said. *It's your birthday?* Dilly nodded. She glanced at the hovering scone plate, the beautifully baked half-wing that Edward wasn't eating. Mummy's laugh whooped out, she'd told a joke, or someone had.

That is very wonderful, Father Muturi said. *We must do a birthday blessing. Oh, yes, marvellous,* said Edward.

Father Muturi cleared his throat noisily, stepped down off the hearth and into the room. He was a big man and when he moved it was seismic. The heads of the guests turned. Father Muturi held out his hands. He waited, professionally, horrifyingly, for attention, and Dilly began to realise what was happening, what was going to happen. One by one the guests fell quiet. Mummy's voice was the last to ring, its notes high, its key pervasively major. She stepped round the guests and came closer, positioned herself at the front. Theatre at a party was her favourite thing.

Father Muturi waggled his fingers a little. Edward had removed himself to the side and Dilly was now, inescapably, the main scene. Everyone's eyes were on her, Mummy's especially, a concentrated, avian glare. Dilly tried to smile, to look game, and humble, ready to receive. She glanced at Cleo for help, but her sister was whispering something in Peter's ear and smirking. Dilly looked down at the floorboards. The dizziness was not airy any more, but heavy, located inside her body. She felt like a weight going down into dark water. In London, she had fainted a few times – low on iron – and been given tablets that tasted nasty and turned everything black. It was quite nice, disappearing for a little while. It would be quite nice now. But, of course, there would be the waking, the being helped up, the fuss, and knowing she had been a spectacle, more of a spectacle than she already was.

Father Muturi set his feet wide apart and placed his hands on Dilly's head. She felt her knees bend and she sank involuntarily. The hands followed her down, made contact again. Dilly tried to stay still. She tried to be present, but it did feel as if she was being towed away. The priest began. *On this very special day, this very special girl who God has given...* He paused. *How many years, please?* He was asking Dilly, or anyone. *Thirty,* called Mummy. *She's thirty!* Then, as an aside, *Lordy, can you believe it, our Dilly!* There were a few claps, though why Dilly didn't know. The pressure of Father Muturi's touch lifted. He made an um-ing noise, and seemed confused. Dilly shut her eyes, waited. Was this bad? She thought of Charlie-bo. His giant robe-like coat. His ruined hazel eyes. His terrible predicament: not the fruit joke, but his life. She thought of Rebecca, pictured her, fatally, like the painting of the goat in the Fitzwilliam with its red headband, standing in salt near the water, its amber eyes dying. She'd taken Sam to see it a few weeks ago. She'd wanted to tell him that this was what happened when you didn't belong any more, when you took the sins of others and were cast out. Like Rebecca. Rebecca was a scapegoat. It was a secret, dangerous thought, not ever to be shared with anyone. And Sam hadn't really been interested in the painting – he'd wanted to see the Samurai masks. Father Muturi touched Dilly's hair again, gently, firmly, and she thought of the river, the river's grace and indifference. She felt the river moving past her, its strong, cold muscles. She felt herself going with it. After a moment the priest spoke, issued some kind of blessing, but Dilly couldn't really hear.

When it was over, the guests went back to chatting and laughing and drinking tea. Dilly sat down on the sofa. For a moment, she felt Mummy's eyes still on her, assessing, but nothing passed between them. Mummy must have sensed, decided not to make the introduction, because Dilly wasn't hoisted over to the magazine woman. Instead, a cup of tea was handed down to her. And then a plate, bearing a whole, uncut scone, with two glistening heaps, white and red, cream and jam. Around the scone was the faded Minton pattern, a ragged botanical tangle. Dilly felt the corner of one eye dampen. Mummy didn't say anything, but the relief, the reprieve, was overwhelming. Her hands were trembling a little as she pushed her thumbs into the soft body of the scone and split it open. She took one big piece and swabbed it through the jam and then through the cream; she lifted it and bit into it. The ducts at the back of her mouth stung and saliva flooded out painfully. She almost gagged. Then the taste came, sweet, wheaty, that safe, wonderful, family taste. Merrick had been wrong. She had tried to be unmoored, tried to live without protections, but the world was full of grotesque, frightening, ridiculous things. It was full of meaningless sorrow and contradiction. Like a sick little baby, with a perfect soul. Here – didn't he see? – they could all help each other. Failure could be forgiven, good things shared. They could all *be* each other. Who you were, really, was who else you were.

It seemed like a miracle to be left alone on the sofa with tea and food, but there she was. The party continued. Dilly ate the scone quickly, a kind of racked, grateful devouring. She licked jam off her finger. She went to the table and took another scone, heaped on cream – no one saw, no one stopped her – and sat back down with her plate. People were talking, sipping tea, having a jolly time, legs and shoes moved here and there. Her brothers and sister and Mummy circulated. The fire began to die. Father Muturi left, maybe for Kenya. He didn't look at her and he made no goodbyes. The front door closed. A minute later the doorbell rang. Dilly looked up at Mummy to see if she should be the one to answer, but Mummy was already en route, adjusting her pale fur stole. Dilly's duties, it seemed, were all suspended.

She heard a muffled discussion at the door, ladies' voices, ups and downs, trills of indistinguishable words. It was longer than the usual welcome-and-coat-off conversation, so perhaps not a party guest. Then she heard Mummy exclaim, shrilly, *gracious, no!* Mummy came back into the lounge with Lillian, who must just have closed the boutique. Lillian was carrying the loveliest-looking package, an immaculate silver box with a huge beige bow, probably for Dilly, because Lillian was very generous and good at remembering. She and Mummy were still talking in low tones, and Dilly heard Mummy say, *well, should I announce it?* Without waiting for a reply, Mummy said loudly, in her speech-giving voice, *everyone. Listen, please, everyone!* The room fell quiet again.

Mummy's expression was now the one related to dreadful news and dismay. An almost operatic gurn. Her brow was deeply rippled, mouth collapsing in the corners. Her hands were held to her chest. *There's been an accident. They've found, well, a body, it seems, just very close to us, down by the weir.* Her eyes were extremely bright; with tears, Dilly realised. Sometimes things did actually make Mummy very upset. There were gasps of surprise and sympathy, and a few comments and questions, *awful, who, when, should Peter go and lend a hand?* Mummy was drawn back into the group, *no, not identified yet,* she was saying, expertly, though she'd known the information only since Lillian had arrived.

Lillian set the present down on the sofa next to Dilly and perched the other side. She had on the same trousers that Dilly was wearing. The front pleat was perfect. Lillian always looked so beautiful. She smiled. *Are you all right, Dilly? Sorry about the bad news.* Dilly smiled too and nodded, looked back at the scone on the plate. *No Sam today? No, not today.* Dilly took another bite. *Oh well, never mind. This is nice.* Lillian's voice fell a little. *I ran into your dad on the way. He said to say happy birthday. Do you think he'll pop in?* Dilly looked up to see who was left at the party. The magazine lady and Cleo were engrossed in conversation. Peter had disappeared and Dominic was holding a bottle of champagne, unsure whether to open it, while Mummy still seemed preoccupied by the trauma.

It was lovely – the wrapping on Lillian's gift, the people here who really loved her, more than Sam ever would have, the second scone, feeling like giddy déjà vu. She already knew everything, could see the body laid out on the towpath, covered by layers and layers of sodden dishevelled rags, a halo of river water leaking around it. The police had cordoned off the scene, and an ambulance was parked up on the road near the punting station. Figures in white medical suits were lifting the yellow tape, stepping underneath, and carefully approaching the lump that had been dragged out of the water. They were kneeling down and gently uncovering the body, peeling off the wet clothes, lifting the heavy wet skirt of the gown away from the face, taking off pieces of rotten fruit, and the red headband, folding back the long, furred ears, and the face underneath, so peaceful and untormented, was hers.

Come Down Heavy

Jack Houston

& what happened was the bread knife's serrations
flashed in the fluorescent lighting of
the Jobcentre Plus & the advisor's
routine smile fell from his face as
Simone pulled with her teeth the
elbow-length lace glove from her free
arm & tried to flick it into the advisor's
face with a movement of her head but
the glove only flapped & landed at the
edge of his desk & slowly slipped down
to disappear into his lap as Simone
began to slash, slash, slash at her now
bare arm; & as the computer monitor,
keyboard, mouse-pad, mouse &
countertop in front of her were flecked
with small, dark beads of blood, the
advisor squealed & pushed his chair
back against the wall, raised his palms

placatory toward Simone's quiet growl, the quaver in his voice betraying the calmness with which he attempted to tell her to please not further hurt herself, do anything stupid, please stop; Jackie, caught in her new friend's story, could picture easy the advisor's need to urinate into his trousers, the blood drying dark on the desk, the screams of the other service-users as the security guards stomped across the worn & grey carpet towards them, the bearing with which Simone wore her black mini-dress & top hat, how she held the knife & yelled into the sparse atmosphere of the job centre; Luna, Jackie's dog, came into the small kitchen, whined, turned on the spot & sat down by the door at the back of the room & Jackie stood to let her out onto the small section of roof the extended back room of the empty pub below them provided; I'd just had enough Simone said & smiled & seemed to expect applause &, receiving some in the way of Jackie's impressed grin, said the two of them should hang out more.

& what happened was Jackie & Simone would take Luna to the small park by Haggerston Station with the overland trains smoothing in & out above their heads on the rails that ran high on the viaduct, a pile of feathers where a pigeon had been got by a fox, a handbag hung on a railing, probably stolen by someone swift & moving through a local pub as Simone & Jackie bonded over a shared love of Neue Deutsche Härte music, other dog owners entering the park & Simone & Jackie watching, tensed, for the tetchiness that would likely explode from Luna at any moment as she circled the new dog just arrived; Simone mentioned she had a small, one-bedroomed council flat, hers & in secure-tenancy, the block set back from Hackney Road on the Tower Hamlets side & Jackie could have the other bedroom, Simone already using & only needing the larger room, telling Jackie it would be better than there, flicking her eyes to where the Belgrave Arms was sat at the other end of a side-street; & Simone asked what happened to your dog?

& what happened was the short answer was some sort of misfortune Jackie had never determined but the longer involved the story of the supported housing Jackie'd been offered a place at being unable to accept pets & so she'd left Luna with friends who swore they would feed her & walk her & cuddle her as if she were their very own dog & Jackie had only left it a month, maybe two, just enough time to settle in her knew situation, just enough time to steady herself on the methadone, feel brave enough to go back to the large & rambling rabbit-warren squat on City Road where every room seemed to hold another trigger or someone she used to use with, or one of the many others who made up the healthy majority of the squat's occupants, creatives of one stripe or another who pitying-disparaging judged her use, only ever expected her to waste her life away on the stuff she'd sworn to them so many times she'd stop, none of them realising how easy they had it: not using always simple if you never wanted to in the first place; & when she did go back, the friends who'd taken Luna in were no longer there, had left no clue as to where they & Luna might be & it was then that Jackie sat heavy in the second-floor kitchen of the second building & burst into tears as Dan sat next to her, a quiet & commiserative hand on her knee, letting Jackie sit on the least broken chair; it had been Dan who'd let her in at the large front door & seemed pleased to see her & was sure Luna was still inside the building somewhere & she should join him in a search through each floor, going in & out of each room regardless of who may or may not have wanted privacy − this a mission that could not be postponed − & as they came out onto the roof the autumnal sun threw itself through the clouds & lit up the surrounding rooftops as they hurried across & down into the connecting building but still they could find no sign of Jackie's dog & as they sat squeezed in between the slightly too large kitchen table & someone's stacked canvasses still replete with the last thing they'd painted on them, Dan mentioned a drink & that this would be what they needed for such a shock & Jackie, too upset to think of saying no, wound up later with Dan & now Tony – & Mikey, who'd gone to pick up the gear they were now smoking to top off the booze, who said Luna hadn't left with Mads & Gareth, where'd she got that from? but he was sure she had gone with Paul & that lot when they'd moved out of the yard & gone to a more outdoorsy site in Lewisham; where exactly? Jackie had asked & being given directions headed straight there, but arrived & unable to find Paul or that lot, or anyone she knew but there was Luna, yapping & happy to see her but now had only one eye & also a man called Bobby who said Luna was his dog & was called Spitzer anyway & no, no one could just take her claiming her as their own, but Jackie went back, travelled the long DLR all the way again & again & again, & one final time taking Tony who on the promise of cider went with her to swear an oath that Luna *was* Jackie's dog, & that he had photos, of the two of them, happier times, together & at this Bobby relented & said fair enough.

& what happened was the squat on City Road
was evicted & Jackie, already having
missed the rent on her supported
housing one month, maybe two, floated
with Dan & Mikey, found herself at the
back of an empty pub in Dalston,
climbing a drainpipe, being helped up
onto a small section of roof; & once her
& Dan had jimmied open the door set
into the wall up there they waited for
the alarm to go off & not hearing
anything, clambered through the gloom
inside, down the dark stairs by the light
of a phone screen to try & open the
door at the front; this now, or at least
soon-to-be their home, with its small &
dirty kitchen, its large bar-area-cum-
front-room filled with salvaged sofas &
Jackie's sharing of one of the three small
bedrooms uncommitted to her
burgeoning sort-of relationship with
Dan.

& what happened was Simone pushed a shopping
trolley down Queensbridge Road with
Jackie following & holding everything
else she could carry round the corner
onto Hackney Road, the sun low &

weather heavy, the haze of traffic stink
filling the cold but still close air around
them as they walked past the barred
windows of the launderette, the
looming hulk of the disused Gala
bingo hall; turning off the main road &
through a car park, past a white van
with Clean Me fingered into its dusty
exterior, a hatchback with rusted
wheels, two crisp packets chasing each
other round & around in a small eddy
of air, they approached the blue
communal door of George Loveless
House, spikes below the plaque that
bore its name, its two wings spread,
uniform blue front doors in rows along
the floors, the bricks clad in – was that
pebble-dash? Jackie wondered as she
dropped one of the reusable Tesco bags,
a few of her clothes spilling onto the
pavement as she struggled to hold onto
the rest of her possessions & stuff the
jumper & the bra back in & pick it
back up & had to skip-jog to catch
Simone; the doors are usually just open
Simone said as she pulled on the large
& largely plexiglass entrance, but you
can buzz up if they're not & anyway I'll

get you a fob cut when I can; the central curled staircase was often used for TV shoots Simone told Jackie as they squeezed the shopping trolley & the bags into the small lift & sent it up ahead of them & climbed the curling stairs that Jackie saw were indeed atmospheric; & Jackie had to think she'd come down a cat, landed, paws to hard tarmac & now able to circle round twice to make a bed & lay down at last as they puffed up to the hard brick interior & glassless airflowslits of the fifth floor & the lift door slowly juttered open at exactly the same time.

& what happened was Simone said she wasn't sure she was really in the mood so Jackie walked the small & darkening park alone, the tower behind her, the fuzzed glow of the thin-strung lamplights guiding her along the narrow concrete path to The Birdcage, where Christine, heavy set but somehow still too thin, brass-blonde affable over her half-empty bottle of rosé, was already sat at a booth against the back wall of the pub asking, as Jackie came in to sit down, what

Jackie might want; as Christine weaved
to the bar to get another, smaller glass
she fluttered a hand toward the table &
told Jackie that was where Jonathan
Ross, the TV celebrity, sat when he
drank... ...is Jonathan Ross's local she
continued as she returned, drained her
glass & refilled them both to the brim &
referred to Jackie's achievements, the
night already close on the street outside,
the smell of yesterday's flower market
still faint in its air & Christine
condescending, telling Jackie to watch
for this: a dangerous place on the long
climb toward recovery: strong, confident
of never, ever going back, not properly,
feeling so strong & confident it's
probably safe, the odd dabble, a little bit,
not too much obviously, but you can
probably chance it, strong & confident
in the knowledge that as you've given it
up you can risk a dabble, a little bit, not
too much, obviously – this way of
thinking was how she had fallen back to
using not so long ago, Christine
seamlessly switching the talk to herself
& her planned move to Bristol, a
Master's Degree, funded by the 'rents

she said sighing, as if everyone faced the
conundrum of trying to get over-caring
parents to stop caring so much: not that
Jackie held any jealousy, not much at
any rate as Christine sighed again, put
her palms down on the table, said you
know, I always enjoyed it, living at
Simone's though I'm not sure it's quite
the right move for you, babes; Jackie
hadn't known Christine knew Simone,
or had lived with her, once, before;
Christine downed the contents of her
glass, nodded her encouragement for
Jackie to do the same & said watch for
Dean, Simone's ex: he's nasty, possessive
& you'll easily find yourself competition
for Simone's affections even though
Simone & him hate each other like you
wouldn't believe; the barman came over
& cleared the table in front of them of
excuse to stay, the pub soft-lit & quiet as
it was only Monday & the usual profit-
staple of nine-to-five bright young
hard-working things not yet feeling it
nearly close enough to the weekend to
start their carousing & Christine winked,
said I've got a little gear: shall we? & as
they returned to Simone's eyes wide &,

Jackie thought, slightly forced welcome,
they sat in Simone's living-room-cum-
bedroom, on the bunk-bed she'd
discovered on the street, taken apart &
squeezed in the lift & re-assembled, top
bunk long gone to make an almost
four-poster, bits of cloth as drapes hung
from the wooden beams that ran above
head-height, aiding with sleep Simone
had said, easier than fitting curtains to
the small windows of the room – the
three of them smoothing their pieces of
tinfoil, rolling tubes from the same,
filling the room with the acrid smell of
melting smack.

& what happened was the sunshine shone from a
brittle sky & washed everything in the
weak spectrum of a January daytime as
the patchy grass ice-crunched underfoot
wherever it was thick enough in the
small scrubby patch of green behind the
flats, between the bushes on one side
that smothered the community centre
& more bushes on the other that grew
through the fence of the under-fives
play area as through the stubby arms of
the single tree & Luna came scampering

from under one of the bushes with a
frisbee, a ring of solid rubber she laid at
Jackie's feet & pushed her shoulders
down & front paws forward, tail wagging
in a frenzy; Jackie picked the ring up &
tossed it to Simone, who threw it back;
& as back & forth & back & forth &
back & forth it flew between the
women, Luna excitedly following the
ring's spinning progress, every inch of
her doggy attention fixed; Simone took
a step back, said she was going to throw
big & as the rubber disc left her flicked
wrist it went up & over Jackie's head,
Luna yap-yapping behind, & lifted on
an updraft from the air being funnelled
around the tower behind them to keep
rising & catch in the stunted bare
branches of the tree; stood below it,
staring up, they sized up the height
they'd have to reach & Jackie went off a
short way & came back to wobble the
longest stick she could find at the tree,
never quite coming anywhere close to
their plaything – the fun of the afternoon
being brought to an unfair & peremptory
close; & as Jackie's eyes were fixed on
the toy caught in the tree, her stick

drooping & dipping unceremoniously,
Simone surprised her, surprised Luna,
too, the dog yapping & pirouetting at
the sight of Simone lifting Jackie from
her knees toward the branches with a
strength neither realized was contained
within her slender frame as the rubber
ring was pinged free.

& what happened was neither Jackie or Simone
knew when Nigel would call to say he
was heading over & give his order;
Nigel worked in the city, for one of the
banks, would arrive wearing his smart
suits & shoes, having spent the day
peering down & out over London
through the thick glass of his office &
needed somewhere safe & hidden from
his wife, his kids, the existence he
would tell them about that was concrete
enough in his telling but still hard to
grasp: the large house out in Kent, his
golf clubs & sports coupé for the
weekend safe in his two-car garage, the
large garden he enjoyed with that
smiling wife & those sun-blushed kids;
not that Simone or Jackie would have
ever tried to dissuade his visiting – he

would buy as much for them again as he would consume himself, an unspoken service charge for using the flat & a merry lift over the dull keep of regularity their scripted methadone & whatever they could pull together between them provided; Jackie was still careful only to smoke, not return to the needle & its too-quick hit but Simone would take her share into the small kitchen at the front of the flat with its windows bare to the walkway beyond & her not caring, preparing her pin, having to lift up her short skirt & pull down her torn tights to get to her femoral, the big thick tunnel of blood that runs down through the saddle of everyone's pelvis so large & round you can hit it again & again & again & never have to worry about it collapsing, or at least almost never & is all that's left to you once you've exhausted the veins in your arms, your hands, your feet & ankles & have neither the gumption nor skill to suck your thumb at a mirror & attempt to hit your jugular.

& what happened was Simone invited Jenny to
roll out a sleeping mat on the floor-
space available in the corner of Simone's
room because Jenny had been Simone's
friend since they'd both lived on the
road & shared a small single-axle caravan
until that single axle had rusted, snapped
& their home was abandoned, pitched
at an angle in the mud in a field
somewhere just outside Bedford & they
both bunked the train to London;
Jenny's two dogs, Millie & Snip, slept
curled up next to her on the floor, & so
Jackie had little choice but to accept
them all, too, even though Millie fought
with Luna & Snip regularly pissed in the
small square of hallway behind the front
door, & even though Jenny had a
conviction hanging over her: the reason
she couldn't return to her own flat &
had to lay the danger of further
consequence for herself, & for Simone
& Jackie out on the floor of the flat with
her near-empty but constantly &
miraculously resurgent aerosol of body
spray & the three different shades of
eyeshadow that seemed to be her only
possessions; three people, three dogs,

squished into the too-small flat or running up & down the small grass below – Millie & Luna bossing the park between them once they'd got to the stage of only rarely fighting with each other, & so what of the risk Millie, being so aggressive, could attack another dog, an adult, or a child; but Jenny's adventures were not to be long in the fresh air of Tower Hamlets: the neighbours on Columbia Road uneasy at either the fact or the attitude of the young woman soliciting sex on their street every evening quickly led to a kerb crawl from the local constabulary & from there to the three Magistrate's presiding smug & straight-laced over her fate, ordering its large iron door to clang shut.

& what happened was there was the need of an address to which something, posted from overseas, could be received & the package already open on the kitchen counter between them, a wall-covering featuring a luridly painted Lord Krishna already pinned to the hallway wall & the Buddhist skull-head trinket already on each of their wrists & several pots of odd-smelling face cream already diluted & dried out again – this the ketamine boiled down to a paste for importation & the offer of a cash amount as thanks for handling the cargo or part of the cargo itself & Jackie & Simone concluding a cut of the delivery, being worth more sold on, would surely lead to them being both richer & able to float like soap bubbles on a summer breeze, luxurious afternoons spread in Simone's room, the sun filtering through the haze of the cigarette smoke from the straight cigarettes they'd easily afford, bodies numb, minds afloat, Rammstein's *Mutter* blasting from the single tinny speaker wired to Simone's CD Walkman & Simone leaning across to tell Jackie over the noise that this was it, this the highest: a pinnacle never to be surpassed; & though they did try to offload it, some of it, going to the few other flats in the block where they knew people who might be interested, asking around their friends, this activity quickly descended to a frantic race as their dips & the dipping & the dipping again into

what was left of their small cut meant
less & less of it remained, more & more
the chance that they would be left with
nothing but a few ill-defined memories.

& what happened was Simone whooped across
the car park in front of the block, the
wheelchair ahead of her clattering up
the kerb to the thin pavement before
the main door & into the building, into
the lift; & pressing their floor's button,
she sang a song that caught in her voice
like an injury & hung in the air of the
lift's slow ascent as she rested all her
weight self-consciously on her left leg,
keeping the weight off the other; & up
in the flat, when Jackie asked, Simone
laughed off the fact of the wheelchair
half-folded & part-blocking the passage
along the thin walkway to each of the
flats beyond, saying she'd stolen it, seen
it in the foyer of the hospital unattended
& thought what a laugh to push it ahead
of her & out of the wrought-iron gates
& all the way back to the flat; & Simone
didn't mention the chairs in the
consultant's waiting room being padded
& far comfier than those you have to sit

on to wait in A&E or for the blood clinic & your little ticketed number to flash up on the LED counter affixed to the wall so you could go in & roll up your sleeve & have the phlebotomist poke around in your arm until they gave up, & neither did she mention that the seats, in the consultant's waiting area, had cushioned back rests also, as if this rear & aft padding were put there to soften up each patient as they waited to hear whatever it was the consultant was going to inform them of, & also she did not mention what she'd thought of the painting on the wall of the consultant's waiting area, whether or not she'd appreciated the two dark brush stokes that represented two lily stalks poking out of a vase, the way it had been painted in pastel upon pastel upon pastel in similar muted institution-blues-&-greens, the same as the walls of the hospital that she knew, or had at least been told once, were painted in such a shade as to keep the people who had to use the hospital calm no matter what news they were about to be given, no matter if they were about to have revealed to them the life-altering prognosis of, say, their right leg's necessary & imminent amputation.

& what happened was Jackie was on her own in the flat when Dean, can of strong cider dented in the grip of his left fist, a groaned slur to every other word, the focus of his eyes at a waver & the care of his children a mystery, careened along the walkway toward the door of the flat to rap his knuckles on the door & wouldn't wait for Jackie to fully open it before he pushed past her without invite, slid along the hallway wall momentarily before righting himself to go straight & ahead into Jackie's room, flopping himself down on the found sofa cushions she used as a bed & peppering her with questions & asking her intentions, as if Jackie were the dashing but mysterious lead man & Simone some debutante at the ball awaiting proposal; his can slipped from his grip & spilled onto the floor as he sat & he didn't apologise, just picked it up again & slurped from it, burped, patted the cushion next to him & told Jackie to come & sit, he wouldn't bite; Jackie looked around the flat for some sort of excuse but not finding one shuffled into the room & perched herself on the furthest cushion as Dean's pissed grin slowly began to slide & he leaned over her, taller & wider & heavier than he'd seemed when she was still standing, the smell of his cider wafting onto Jackie from his breath, his pores, as he began to say that he would teach her a lesson, that she would be sorry; & Jackie could feel her heart beating in her chest as she leant forward, poised on one bent leg, ready to leap for the door, to scrabble & claw her way past & out as Dean began to sink back, the cushion rolling him into the wall as he said he really would teach Simone a lesson, would take Dermot & Kirsty to Wales, to his mum's & his Nanny Davies he said, & Jackie was still holding her breath as Dean started to cry & said none of them would look back, ever look back, they would forget her & no he didn't care if Simone couldn't get there, didn't care that Wales was as Argentina, Thailand, Siberia, as it was all Simone's fault anyway; & as he listed crimes, some awful, some understandable, Jackie edged toward the door, still unsure of her safety, knowing she couldn't force him from the flat, that she was too scared to even ask him to leave, hoping he'd get bored & sail off under his own propulsion, which he did, eventually, weaving out of the front door & down the walkway, calling over his shoulder how it had been nice to meet her but he didn't trust her & that he hoped her & Simone would be happy together as they were both dirty whores.

& what happened was Jackie had started to slide into the samsara of waking with withdrawals already & trying to squeeze through the day without using too much or just merrily blowing entire giros & whatever came her way, consuming the money that she could have put to better use on food & other provisions in a matter of minutes – all held together by the too-scant administration of their respective methadone scripts, & as there was still a little of the ketamine left to sell,

Simone thought to invite Grant, a friend who Jenny had introduced her to, from a non-specific block across the way, into the flat with a mind to do some sort of deal, but in the fuss of the sale that fell through anyway Simone went to make tea, & Jackie was distracted by another line of k, & Grant left with his excuses for them to discover the bottle of methadone Simone kept down the side of her bed gone, more than a week's supply; dammit Simone said as she punched the wall, leaving three holes in the plaster where her rings had been & then her phone began to ring, & though Jackie went into the kitchen she could still hear her friend saying over & over, no, you can't do that, no, no, no, you can't already be gone, no, you must come back, & no, I don't care if you're already calling from Rhyl; & Jackie heard her friend's sobs as she hung up the phone & went into her & held her in her arms & Jackie knew she would need to do something to take the edge off, to smooth out the night.

& what happened was Jackie split what methadone she had between herself & Simone but this dose would never be enough, halved over the eleven days until Simone received more; Jackie suggested calling Nigel, telling him of their predicament, asking if he could help or just visit but Simone said no, he'd always made clear that to approach him would be to sabotage the fragile politeness of their arrangement, & so they shuffled the length of a sodium-glow Hackney Road, an ache pressing into their limbs that made every step of the short walk an arduous slog, to the fancy bag shop by Cambridge Heath Station & its rows of leather & suede & shiny-buckled bags clearly visible through the window Simone & Jackie had walked past so many times while admiring what must be, Simone had said to Jackie on a blustery afternoon not two weeks earlier, hundreds of pounds worth of merchandise; the crowbar's strike had the window cascade down around them in a thousand diamond-like pieces as the alarm bell threw its hollow clang into the air of Hackney Road & Simone handed Jackie one of the bags from the display & took one herself, reached in to grab more as the twirling blue light turned the corner from Mare Street & they scattering the bags across the pavement, slipping down the back streets to wiggle their way through & away from the constable's hollered entreaties.

& what happened was they spent the next morning either side of the Tesco Express, cross-legged & patient, Jackie leaning on Luna & Simone on Millie, Snip too frail to be brought out as the two women shivered, tried to hold the gaze of each person who came in & out of the shop, most of whom turned away, some of whom at least acknowledging their existence, but this of no merit if it did not lead to a rattle of coins into the used paper cups they'd picked up outside the coffee shop further along the road; after nearly an hour Jackie couldn't feel Luna on her legs anymore, looked across but Simone was talking to someone who was reaching into his shopping bag to hand over a useless sandwich that

Jackie hoped would at least be shared, knowing she dared not move away in case that was the moment someone would shimmer from the door of the Tesco in an apparition of generosity & throw at her a whole pound; but as another person walked out still filling their plastic bag with affordable goods while staring hard at a spot of pavement that was anywhere but directly at the one Jackie was uncomfortable & sat at: excuse me, love, have you got...? Jackie began to feel the word No screw itself somewhere deep inside herself, Sorry become a part of who she was.

& what happened was they were back inside the flat, standing in front of a lit oven, trying to get warm again & Simone clutched at her midriff, lolled across the hall to the small bathroom & vomited, hard, into the bath & voided her bowels into her knickers & Jackie said okay, stay here, I'll find something.

& what happened was when Jackie jangled out to try & find something, anything, Simone ignored the barking of the three hungry dogs & stepped over a small pile of Snip's shit & picked up one of the dog leads that was slung over the small radiator in the hallway & back in her room placed the small speaker by the frame to her bed & wrapped the length of rope carefully over the beam of the missing top bunk & held each end & pulled down on it to test the beam's strength & then threaded the lead through its own hand-hold & around the beam & affixed the spring clip to the dog lead itself & placing a hand in the loop she had made, pulled down, the noose tightening against her fist, the clip digging into her fingers & knuckles whitening & fingertips reddening as she lifted her heels ever so slightly from the floor.

& what happened was it was only twenty, thirty minutes later that Jackie came back in breathless & excited, said I've got something, I've got something, & had to shush the dogs that were frenzied at her feet; she had walked out into the cold blast of February at the bottom of the flats & there: a wallet sat calm &

unclaimed on the tarmac of the car park, having surely fallen from the pocket of someone getting into a car & driving away & leaving their leather-held bounty to await Jackie's grasp; & as the dealer pulled into the car-park to see Jackie, huddled against the bin-shed, knees up & arms crossed & face down, he had to sound his horn two, three times to alert her to the fact that he was there; & as she bounded up the spiralled stairs, no need for the lift, a new & unstoppable energy flushed through her, brought to her with the possession of what was in her hand & she opened the door of the flat & ignored the strenuous barking of the three dogs & popped her head round Simone's door & said I got something, I got something, & Simone was there, by her bed, & Jackie rushed into the kitchen to grab the foil from the kitchen drawer & the Martell-bottle pipe from where it was sat next to the kettle & came back through & Simone still exactly where she had been & Jackie said Simone? & saw that Simone's head was hung, awkward, that something was holding the bend of Simone's neck to the top beam of the bunk, her feet not quite to the floor & Jackie pulled Simone's hair away & saw & tried to unclip the dog lead but the rope was stretched too taught, the clasp too firmly dug into her friend's neck & she tried to lift her to let it loosen but couldn't so crashed back through to the kitchen & grabbed the bread knife from the drawer & went back & slashed & slashed & slashed at the lead & her friend fell forward blue-lipped & bruise-eyed but still warm & came down heavy, collapsing on top of Jackie who fell back against the threadbare carpet & held her & held her & held her.

Scrimshaw

Eley Williams

AND AGAIN WE WERE messaging late at night until the early hours of the morning. I pressed my face closer to my phone screen and imagined you doing the same. A whole town stretched between us, and I considered the surface of our separate skins blued or bluewn or bluesed by pixel-light as we typed against our own private darknesses.

We dispatched small talk, sweet talk. Sweet nothings. Then your message said that you were feeling unhappy. *We're all feeling unhappy,* I thought but also flushed with responsibility for taking charge of your state of mind. I flexed my thumbs.

I couldn't ask you about your day because perhaps that had been the cause of your unhappiness and would just further it. I couldn't tell you about my day because it was the cause of my unhappiness and might exacerbate your own. I couldn't comment on the weather or the politics or the price of either and neither of those things because unhappiness *unhappiness* unhappiness. I kept typing the first letter of possible responses to you even though I know that this causes three rippling dots to appear on your phone screen. These dots change in character depending on your mood: ellipses, Hansel and Gretel breadcrumbs, Polyphemus' sockets, the side of a rolled dice. As I trialled potential first responder letters, the trailing three dots must be shifting minutely on your phone screen. Three dots undulating while I dithered, modulating the colour of the blue light hitting your face as you waited for my message to materialise. I drafted a breath then deleted it.

The word *unhappy* implies something of a void. A state of *not-happiness*, sure, but not necessarily one featuring a person in an active participation of despair. I looked up synonyms for *unhappiness* and wondered where on the scale you might place yourself if given the option: *cheerlessness, desolation, despair, despondency, dolefulness, downheartedness, gloom, gloominess, glumness, malaise, wretchedness.* I would list them to you in alphabetical order like this so to not imply my own personal hierarchy in terms of the terms.

Perhaps best not to dwell on the word *unhappiness.* 'You cannot be in control of another person's feelings,' was a phrase I had once overheard on a bus. It spoke to me. It resonated, and I thought to save it to my Notes on my phone and embolden the text. So: no need to draw attention to your unhappiness by querying it or requesting context: I cannot hope to lance that boil for you without first dragging out descriptions of the boil, handling the boil, prodding the boil and haranguing it unto carbuncles. This metaphor has run away with me to the fair. What I mean is: questions, as with boils, can cause irritation from direct pressure and over time the inflamed area enlarges. Better then to dwell apart from your unhappiness in my answer. *You cannot be in control of another person's feelings.* Undwell, antidwell, disdwell, dedwell.

I send you a link to an online live-feed of walruses.

The page was a go-to site for me. I had it bookmarked, ready for whenever insomnia had me in its grip or its jaws or its jar or its spackle. The walrus live-feed is maintained by the Alaska Department of Fish & Game with their cameras trained 24/7 on the Walrus Islands State Game Sanctuary *(WISGS),* one of the largest gathering places in the world for Pacific Walruses. Whenever the season is right at any time of day or night you can click on to the live-stream and watch 15,000 walruses rolling about and sunning themselves. Puffy and hairy and taking stock of their walrus days. There is audio too which just adds to the charm: your phone or laptop speakers come alive with their huffing and puffing, moustach_eod blurts and blusterings of no-foot never-footed scuffling.

I think walruses belong to that sub-set of animals that are twee but also somehow noble in their anatomical absurdity. They look like they were designed for the purposes of an Edward Lear poem. See also: penguins, pelicans, flamingos, koalas. Maybe that's a personal opinion. I should list them to you in alphabetical order so to not imply a hierarchy: *flamingos, koalas, pelicans, penguins, walruses.* Walruses look frustrated and benign. I thought that this might be an appropriate response to your unhappiness: I am sorry for frustrations, you were right to tell me, I can be your technique for distraction. I can never tell if we are flirting but I can help you. *I can distract you,* I draft. I delete. *I want to drive you to distraction,* I try typing. No. Dot dot dot. *I love you,* I draft in my text message, a word for each dot that must appear on your phone's screen. I delete the draft.

On idle instinct, I click the link that I sent to you. I want to check what was currently taking place at WISGS walrus colony. I could use the distraction too. The page begins to load: *REFRESHING STREAM* it reads. Soon, I think: walruses in a refreshing stream.

I give a pleased sigh and draw my phone closer to my face, twitching my thumb and reading facts about walruses in case my link acted as an opener for further conversation between us. In terms of taxonomy, the family name for walruses is *Odobenidae*. I think that's one of those words that has the same shape as its meaning. Another one of these words is bed. You can see what I mean in lowercase: *bed*. You can see the headboard and the footrest and a little plumping of duvet there. Maybe *llama* is another one: the shape of the word looks like a llama sitting down, its legs tucked beneath its body. Just so, *Odobenidae* is a walrus lying, merman aslant, on its side. I consider typing all this to you but want to make sure you have responded to the link first. Maybe it will take a while for you to work out what I've sent you. Perhaps your connection is poor. I thumb through more facts as a distraction technique.

Nobody seems to have a clear idea of the word *walrus'* etymology. Surely it's unlikely to be related to some notional 'horse-whale', a rearrangement of its aquequine parts through language. I skip along some bluish screens and read that 'a variety of walrus found in the North Pacific has sometimes received the distinct specific name *obesus*'. I roll in my bed and chew the cud of that fact. *You cannot be in control of another person's feelings.* Another site claims that a name given to the ivory of their tusks is *morse*. It shows small objects, crucifixes and jewellery made from sawn tuskbone. More. Cryptic and coded in their fatheadedness, *Odobenidae* morsey and moreish, their rubber faces standing up on wealthy white stilts.

You have not replied. It has been minutes. Usually you are quicker than this. My phone tells me it's 4:02 which doesn't look like the shape of anything. I check to see what is happening on the live-feed of walruses, relieved to see that the page has finally loaded. I would not have wanted to send you a dead link, down a dead-end.

The walruses on my screen are grey and pink. They are brawling. No, they are not brawling. They are roaring as they not-brawl.

I realise I have sent you a link to a live-stream of walruses mating. It is obscenely in High Definition, as obscene and absurd and rolling and violent and loafish as 4:02 on a clock face and I have never been more awake in my life.

I wait and wait. The walruses mate on. I draft an apology then delete and wait and wait and I am so unhappy, *dejected,* wretched. There are no three dots from you in answer, not even the beginning of an SOS because you have fallen asleep? switched your phone off? ceased to exist entirely? All three. I concentrate on ceasing to exist entirely but I do not know what you are thinking, *we cannot be in control of another person's feelings,* but I did not mean to send that to you, and I hope the thrill of error filled your state of not-happiness, and know there is a blue glow between my fingers, my fist over my screen, and the sound of braying, and lancing, remorseful, like something loud and long and clear.

About the Authors

Caleb Azumah Nelson is a 26-year-old British–Ghanaian writer and photographer living in South East London. His writing has been published in *Litro* and is forthcoming in *The White Review*. He was recently shortlisted for the Palm Photo Prize and won the People's Choice prize. *Open Water*, forthcoming with Penguin Viking (UK) and Grove Atlantic (US) is his first novel.

Jan Carson is a writer and community arts facilitator based in East Belfast. Her debut novel *Malcolm Orange Disappears* and short story collection, *Children's Children,* were published by Liberties Press, Dublin. A micro-fiction collection, *Postcard Stories* was published by the Emma Press in 2017. A second volume is forthcoming in August 2020. Her novel *The Fire Starters* was published by Doubleday in April 2019 and subsequently won the EU Prize for Literature for

Ireland 2019, the Blackwell's Books Kitschies Prize for speculative fiction and was shortlisted for the inaugural Dalkey Book Prize 2020. She has also been shortlisted for the Sean O'Faolain Short Story Prize and in 2016 won the Harper's Bazaar Short Story Prize. Her work has appeared in journals such as *Banshee, The Tangerine* and *Winter Papers,* and on BBC Radio 3 and 4.

Sarah Hall was born in Cumbria in 1974. Twice nominated for the Man Booker Prize, she is the award-winning author of five novels and three short-story collections – *The Beautiful Indifference,* which won the Edge Hill and Portico prizes, *Madame Zero,* shortlisted for the Edge Hill Prize and winner of the East Anglian Book Award, and *Sudden Traveller* (2019). She is currently the only author to be three times shortlisted for the BBC National Short Story Award, which she won in 2013 with 'Mrs Fox'.

Jack Houston is a writer from London. His poetry has been published in a wide range of literary magazines and in a few anthologies, been shortlisted for the Basil Bunting and Keats-Shelley Prizes and taken second prize in the 2017 Poetry London Competition. He works within Hackney's Libraries where he has held a range of poetry events, most recently an online Lockdown Poetry Workshop. He also teaches a poetry writing course for a local chapter of Age UK. As a mature student, he received a BA in Creative Writing from London Metropolitan University and then went on to receive an MA in Writing Poetry from Newcastle University.

Eley Williams lectures at Royal Holloway, University of London. Her short story collection *Attrib. and Other Stories* (Influx Press) won the James Tait Black Prize and the Republic of Consciousness Prize. *The Liar's Dictionary* (William Heinemann) is her debut novel and is published this year.

About the BBC National Short Story Award with Cambridge University

The BBC National Short Story Award is one of the most prestigious for a single short story and celebrates the best in home-grown short fiction. The ambition of the award, which is now in its fifteenth year, is to expand opportunities for British writers, readers and publishers of the short story, and honour the UK's finest exponents of the form. The award is a highly regarded feature within the literary landscape with a justified reputation for genuinely changing writers' careers.

James Lasdun secured the inaugural award in 2006 for 'An Anxious Man'. Jumping to 2012, when the Award expanded internationally for one year to mark the London Olympics, the Bulgarian writer Miroslav Penkov was victorious with his story 'East of the West'. In more recent years, we've seen a trend towards writers who are 'earlier' in their writing journeys coming through to the shortlist and winning. Following her win in 2018, Ingrid Persaud signed with Rogers Coleridge White literary agency after being courted by multiple agents, and went on to sell her debut novel *Love After Love* to Faber & Faber in a seven-way auction. 2019 winner Jo Lloyd has also signed with an agent and is working towards publishing a collection of short stories. Other alumni include Lionel Shriver, Zadie Smith, Hilary Mantel, Sarah Hall, Jon McGregor, Rose Tremain and William Trevor.

The winning author receives £15,000, and four further shortlisted authors £600 each. All five shortlisted stories are broadcast on BBC Radio 4 along with interviews with the writers.

In 2015, to mark the National Short Story Award's tenth anniversary, the BBC Young Writers' Award was launched in order to inspire the next generation of short story writers, to raise the profile of the form with a younger audience, and provide an outlet for their creative labours. The teenage writers shortlisted for the award have their stories recorded by professional actors and broadcast, plus they are interviewed on-air and in the media. The winner of the 2019 award was 16-year-old Georgie Woodhead with her story 'Jelly-headed'.

To inspire the next generation of short story readers, teenagers around the UK are also involved in the BBC National Short Story Award via the BBC Student Critics' Award, which gives selected 16- to 18-year-olds the opportunity to read, listen to, discuss and critique the five stories shortlisted by the judges, and have their say. The students are supported with discussion guides, teaching resources and interactions with writers and judges, for an enriching experience that brings literature to life.

The year 2018 marked the start of an exciting collaboration between the BBC and the University of Cambridge and First Story. The University of Cambridge supports all three awards, and hosts a range of short story events at the Institute of Continuing Education, which offers a range of creative writing and English Literature programmes, and curates an exclusive online exhibition of artefacts drawn from the University Library's archive to inspire and intrigue entrants of the Young Writers' Award. The charity First Story bring their experience in fostering creativity, confidence and writing skills in secondary schools serving low-income communities to bear, by supporting the Young Writers' Award and the Student Critics' Award with activity engaging young people with reading, writing and listening to short stories.

For more information on the awards, please visit www.bbc.co.uk/nssa and www.bbc.co.uk/ywa. You can also keep up-to-date on Twitter via #BBCNSSA, #BBCYWA and #shortstories

Award Partners

BBC Radio 4 is the world's biggest single commissioner of short stories, which attract more than a million listeners. Contemporary stories are broadcast every week, the majority of which are specially commissioned throughout the year.

www.bbc.co.uk/radio4

BBC Radio 1 is the UK's No.1 youth station, targeting 15- to 29-year-olds with a distinctive mix of new music and programmes focusing on issues affecting young people. The station is the soundtrack to young people's lives in the UK and has been for over 50 years.

www.bbc.co.uk/radio1

The mission of the **University of Cambridge** is to contribute to society through the pursuit of education, learning and research at the highest international levels of excellence. To date, 107 affiliates of the University have won the Nobel Prize. Founded in 1209, the University comprises

31 autonomous Colleges, which admit undergraduates and provide small-group tuition, and 150 departments, faculties and institutions. The University sits at the heart of one of the world's largest technology clusters. The 'Cambridge Phenomenon' has created 1,500 hi-tech companies, 14 of them valued at over US$1 billion and two at over US$10 billion. Cambridge promotes the interface between academia and business and has a global reputation for innovation. The BBC National Short Story Award is being supported by the School of Arts and Humanities, Faculty of English, University Library and the new University of Cambridge Centre for Creative Writing which is part of the University of Cambridge Institute of Continuing Education, which provides a range of part-time and full-time courses to members of the public. www.ice.cam.ac.uk/centre-creative-writing

First Story believes there is dignity and power in being able to tell your own story, and that writing can transform lives. We're working towards a society that encourages and supports all young people to write creatively for pleasure and agency. We're committed to bringing opportunities for creativity to students who may not otherwise have the chance. Our flagship programme places professional writers into secondary schools serving low-income communities, where they work intensively with students and teachers to foster confidence, creativity and writing ability. Through our core programme and extended activities, we expand young people's horizons and raise aspirations. Participants gain vital skills that underpin academic attainment and support achieving potential. Find out more and get involved at www.firststory.org.uk

Interview with Di Speirs

Di Speirs is the Books Editor for BBC Radio and has produced numerous editions of Book at Bedtime over two decades and the first ever Book of the Week in 1998. She has been instrumental in the internationally acclaimed BBC National Short Story Award since its inception in 2006. She is a member of the Charleston Small Wonder Lifetime's Excellence in Short Fiction Award panel.

The BBC National Short Story Award launched in 2005. What is the most surprising thing you have learnt about short fiction (or running a prestigious national award) in that time?

Maybe it's not surprising, but it's certainly confirmed to me how very difficult it is to write short fiction well. There's so much out there that's perfectly competent and quite enjoyable, but to really echo over time, a story requires a focus and brilliance that's very hard to achieve.

As far as running the award goes, I've discovered a wonderful community of writers and lovers of short fiction, and realised that we can make a genuine difference to writers' lives and the profile of the form, despite the competition for space and eyeballs. The power of audio, of course, has always been clear to those of us who live and breathe radio – what is nicer than being read to? And knowing over a million people will hear each of the stories on BBC Radio 4 and via BBC Sounds is still something I take great pride in.

What is the most invigorating part of the BBC NSSA judging process for you? And the most challenging?
Every year, the most exciting element of judging is discovering new voices I didn't know, being told a story in a new way that lingers long after or finding out that writers I already love can do something surprisingly different. As we read blind, it's also fun finding out that a story I like is by someone unexpected, whose identity I hadn't guessed.

Identifying the themes in the content that are rising to the surface every year is always fascinating. These change by some unquantifiable magic to do with the zeitgeist, but almost every year, there is a theme or two that bubbles up – sometimes we travel far and wide, sometimes it's much more British-based. Short stories respond to our circumstances quickly. In 2019, there was much more fantastical writing, from magic to folklore – perhaps reflecting the difficulties of the current divisions and turbulent times that we are living in. A number of stories were making a plea, however disguised, for tolerance. In the 2020 shortlist, we have bold new voices tackling tough realities and incisive humour within domestic tensions, reflecting a generation of writers playing with form, range and the freedom of short fiction.

The most challenging aspect of judging is to give myself the space to read, not least because I'm also reading so much else for work. I've learnt over the years to pace myself and not read too many stories at once. They need air around them or they become indistinguishable, and occasionally indigestible! And that's when you can miss a gem, through saturation.

The other huge challenge is keeping it all going – finding partners in a challenging landscape, not least for the BBC. I believe very passionately that we make a substantial difference to writers' careers and the wider support for the publication and reading of short stories – so while it's never easy, it's absolutely worth fighting to keep such a cherished award afloat.

For more than a decade, you have championed the short story form. Where does your love of fiction and, in particular, short fiction, stem from?

My love of fiction began as a very young child being read to by both my parents – who remain great readers themselves, to this day. It explains perhaps why I loved making *Book at Bedtime* for so many years, being read to is in my blood. As a child, I discovered books weekly in the Blackhall library in Edinburgh, and powered through them. Short stories took me longer to appreciate. A friend at university gave me William Trevor's *The Ballroom of Romance*, which remains a deeply treasured, if battered, collection, and I've never looked back. I discovered then that great short stories fed me and took me elsewhere very powerfully, and I've loved them ever since.

It's an impossible question to answer, but what makes a great short story for you – what do you in particular enjoy and look for when selecting winners?

I want to be drawn in, intrigued, to find myself uncovering layers of a story, but that can be done in so many ways; themes threaded together, depth of a character, or a story that reaches back in time, while casting forward. It's critical to believe in the world that's drawn and to be engaged with characters, but I'm also always looking for originality of form and really outstanding writing. And I must be able to excavate more deeply on a second and third read – so many stories have given their all in the first hit.

I particularly like short stories with an emotional impact – Kate Clanchy's 'The Not-Dead and the Saved' remains one of my all-time favourite winners of the award; Sarah Hall's 'Mrs Fox' was an outstanding example of sublime writing that subverted the expected.

Are there any themes or phrases or styles that you think are woefully overdone in the world of short fiction? Anything you would happily not see on paper again?

There's a lot of rather *overwriting* that would be so much better pared back. Coming-of-age is hard to do originally and there are sometimes too many stories about the lost, but I'm loathe to be prescriptive, because no subject should be off-limits and anything can be written about well. In 2019, we had a lot of stories including both selkies (seal-women) and middle-aged women living in sad circumstances by the shore (from the Highlands to Kent) – which, while good, possibly missed out because we felt we were returning to the same trope. Next year, I expect we'll receive a lot of stories about global pandemics. More positively, I'd like to see more experimentation with form, more comedic writing – that's so rare – and more stories reflecting the lives of the young today.

The BBC NSSA is famous for its all-female shortlists. Apparently, submissions from female writers tend to account for 50–70% of your submissions. With that in mind, what are the challenges facing female writers in today's industry, would you say?

The six all-female shortlists are testament to how women in particular are hugely confident with short stories and prepared to take risks and to invest in them – you can see it in wonderful collections from many of our winning and shortlisted writers, from Sarah Hall to KJ Orr, Clare Wigfall to Lionel Shriver. I think we need to turn the question on its head and ask why fewer men are entering – are they intimidated?! Or is it seen as a less viable form?

I don't really think that's the case: think of the writers such as Jon McGregor, Colin Barrett, Kevin Barry, Tom Morris and David Szalay who are writing superb short fiction. What might be true is that for those nervous of committing to a whole novel because their lives are full, maybe short fiction seems more achievable – but, of course, it isn't actually easier, and it's certainly still harder to make any sort of living from it.

I'm very encouraged by the greater investment in and prominence of short story collections now than 15 years ago – but there's a long way to go. And we need more places such as Radio 4 and the excellent literary magazines to invest in the writers and help them to hone their craft and eat at the same time.

What more do you think can be done to encourage new and diverse voices to submit their work to competitions?
Spreading the word remains crucial, but I am encouraged by the change in the demographic over 15 years. We have a much wider spread of submissions than we did at the start and we hope that by publicising that fact, we continue to help break down the sense that there are barriers. It's free to enter, which should help wider representation. Entrants do need to have had published one piece of creative writing – that can be a poem or a play, as well as short or long fiction – so we are trying to find people who have put some time into writing.

But the 2018 winner, Ingrid Persaud, entered with her first-ever story 'The Sweet Sop' – and won! – so anything can happen. I always like to see younger writers entering and hope that one day soon we'll start to see entries from the amazing people who enter our Young Writers' Award for those age 13 and 18 – something you can enter without any publishing record. On a broader note, the industry is changing, too slowly, but there's a rise in the amount of fiction being published from a more diverse range of voices. I hope that will continue to feed in to the awards.

What tips or advice would you offer writers of short stories who are looking for competition success? Editing, tone, dialogue, bravery, etc?

My biggest tip is edit. Not once, but again and again. It's the worst short story cliché, but there isn't room for wasted words, and the best short stories are spare and pinpoint sharp.

They have to have something to say so being brave is important, too. I don't mind about dialogue (though there's no doubt it helps on air in particular – although that isn't a judging criteria for the award), but the story needs to stand up to multiple re-readings – both by yourself as the author, finessing and killing your darlings, and from judges who need to find more as they dive in.

Of course, read great short stories – old and new – and see what they are doing. Also be playful, take a risk, don't explain everything, assume your reader is intelligent and will take a leap of faith, be imaginative, don't be afraid to portray kindness or to be still, in the moment, but avoid the overly lyrical, the overly sentimental and the overly overwritten!

What are your hopes for the coming years for the BBC NSSA? And for short fiction (in general) in the future...
I hope, despite Covid-19 and the challenges it has brought to all our lives, that our 15th award will be even more widely heard, read and enjoyed and that our listeners and readers will go back to previous stories, too, and that all five of the writers, whoever they turn out to be, will find it a springboard into a writing career if they are at the beginning – or a valued appreciation and addition to their work if they are long established.

From then, I hope we can head smoothly towards our 20th and beyond, helping to celebrate a great form.

There are many reasons why we need short fiction and the short form more than ever now – and the blends of creative non-fiction and auto-fiction, the rise in the essay, especially in the States, underline that. When attention spans are challenged, and much as you might want a long escape into a novel, it's hard to achieve sometimes; a story still offers the chance to inhabit another world, feel another's pain – or love, and can resonate more powerfully and for longer than its limited word count initially suggests. The world would be a much poorer place without short fiction.

Interview by Sophie Haydock
First published by The Sunday Times Audible Short Story Award

Previous Winners

2019: 'The Invisible' by Jo Lloyd

2018: 'The Sweet Sop' by Ingrid Persaud

2017: 'The Edge of the Shoal' by Cynan Jones

2016: 'Disappearances' by KJ Orr
Runner-up: 'Morning, Noon & Night'
by Claire-Louise Bennett

2015: 'Briar' by Jonathan Buckley
Runner-up: 'Bunny' by Mark Haddon

2014: 'Kilifi Creek' by Lionel Shriver
Runner-up: 'Miss Adele Amidst the Corsets'
by Zadie Smith

2013: 'Mrs Fox' by Sarah Hall
Runner-up: 'Notes from the House Spirits'
by Lucy Wood

2012: 'East of the West' by Miroslav Penkov
Runner-up: 'Sanctuary' by Henrietta Rose-Innes

2011: 'The Dead Roads' by D W Wilson
Runner-up: 'Wires' by Jon McGregor

2010: 'Tea at the Midland' by David Constantine
Runner-up: 'If It Keeps On Raining'
by Jon McGregor

2009: 'The Not-Dead & the Saved' by Kate
Clanchy
Runner-up: 'Moss Witch' by Sara Maitland

2008: 'The Numbers' by Clare Wigfall
Runner-up: 'The People on Privilege Hill'
by Jane Gardam

2007: 'The Orphan and the Mob' by Julian Gough
Runner-up: 'Slog's Dad' by David Almond

2006: 'An Anxious Man' by James Lasdun
Runner-up: 'The Safehouse' by Michel Faber

BBC NATIONAL SHORT STORY AWARD 2020